Skipping Christmas

John
Grisham

....

DOUBLEDAY   *New York   London   Toronto   Sydney   Auckland*

Skipping Christmas

PUBLISHED BY DOUBLEDAY
a division of Random House, Inc.
1540 Broadway, New York, New York 10036

DOUBLEDAY and the portrayal of an anchor with a dolphin are
trademarks of Doubleday, a division of Random House, Inc.

Book design by Maria Carella

Library of Congress Cataloging-in-Publication Data applied for

ISBN 0-385-50841-7 (Hardcover)
ISBN 0-375-43162-4 (Large Print)
ISBN 0-385-50624-4 (Limited Edition)

November 2001
First Edition
1   3   5   7   9   10   8   6   4   2

Skipping Christmas

One

....

The gate was packed with weary travelers, most of them standing and huddled along the walls because the meager allotment of plastic chairs had long since been taken. Every plane that came and went held at least eighty passengers, yet the gate had seats for only a few dozen.

There seemed to be a thousand waiting for the 7 P.M. flight to Miami. They were bundled up and heavily laden, and after fighting the traffic and the check-in and the mobs along the concourse they were subdued, as a whole. It was the Sunday after Thanksgiving, one of the busiest days of the year for air travel, and as they jostled and got pushed farther into the gate many asked themselves, not for the first time, why, exactly, they had chosen this day to fly.

The reasons were varied and irrelevant at the moment. Some tried to smile. Some tried to read, but the crush and the noise made it difficult. Others just stared at the floor and waited. Nearby a skinny black Santa Claus clanged an irksome bell and droned out holiday greetings.

A small family approached, and when they saw the gate number and the mob they stopped along the edge of the concourse and began their wait. The daughter was young and pretty. Her name was Blair, and she was obviously leaving. Her parents were not. The three gazed at the crowd, and they, too, at that moment, silently asked themselves why they had picked this day to travel.

The tears were over, at least most of them. Blair was twenty-three, fresh from graduate school with a handsome résumé but not ready for a career. A friend from college was in Africa with the Peace Corps, and this had inspired Blair to dedicate the next two years to helping others. Her assignment was eastern Peru, where she would teach primitive little children how to read. She would live in a lean-to with no plumbing, no electricity, no phone, and she was anxious to begin her journey.

The flight would take her to Miami, then to Lima, then by bus for three days into the mountains, into another century. For the first time in her young and sheltered life, Blair would spend Christmas away from home. Her mother clutched her hand and tried to be strong.

The good-byes had all been said. "Are you sure this is what you want?" had been asked for the hundredth time.

Luther, her father, studied the mob with a scowl on his face. What madness, he said to himself. He had dropped them at the curb, then driven miles to park in a satellite lot. A packed shuttle bus had delivered him back to Departures, and from there he had elbowed his way with his wife and daughter down to this gate. He was sad that Blair was leaving, and he detested the swarming horde of people. He was in a foul mood. Things would get worse for Luther.

The harried gate agents came to life and the passengers inched forward. The first announcement was made, the one asking those who needed extra time and those in first class to come forward. The pushing and shoving rose to the next level.

"I guess we'd better go," Luther said to his daughter, his only child.

They hugged again and fought back the tears. Blair smiled and said, "The year will fly by. I'll be home next Christmas."

Nora, her mother, bit her lip and nodded and kissed her once more. "Please be careful," she said because she couldn't stop saying it.

"I'll be fine."

They released her and watched helplessly as she joined a long line and inched away, away from them, away from home and security and everything she'd ever known. As she handed over her boarding pass, Blair turned and smiled at them one last time.

"Oh well," Luther said. "Enough of this. She's going to be fine."

Nora could think of nothing to say as she watched her daughter disappear. They turned and fell in with the foot traffic, one long crowded march down the concourse, past the Santa Claus with the irksome bell, past the tiny shops packed with people.

It was raining when they left the terminal and found the line for the shuttle back to the satellite, and it was pouring when the shuttle sloshed its way through the lot and dropped them off, two hundred yards from their car. It cost Luther $7.00 to free himself and his car from the greed of the airport authority.

When they were moving toward the city, Nora finally spoke. "Will she be okay?" she asked. He had heard that question so often that his response was an automatic grunt.

"Sure."

"Do you really think so?"

"Sure." Whether he did or he didn't, what did it matter at this point? She was gone; they couldn't stop her.

He gripped the wheel with both hands and silently cursed the traffic slowing in front of him. He couldn't tell if his wife was crying or not. Luther wanted only to get home and dry off, sit by the fire, and read a magazine.

He was within two miles of home when she announced, "I need a few things from the grocery."

"It's raining," he said.

"I still need them."

"Can't it wait?"

"You can stay in the car. Just take a minute. Go to Chip's. It's open today."

So he headed for Chip's, a place he despised not only for its outrageous prices and snooty staff but also for its impossible location. It was still raining of course—she couldn't pick a Kroger where you could park and make a dash. No, she wanted Chip's, where you parked and hiked.

Only sometimes you couldn't park at all. The lot was full. The fire lanes were packed. He searched in vain for ten minutes before Nora said, "Just drop me at the curb." She was frustrated at his inability to find a suitable spot.

He wheeled into a space near a burger joint and demanded, "Give me a list."

"I'll go," she said, but only in feigned protest. Luther would hike through the rain and they both knew it.

"Gimme a list."

"Just white chocolate and a pound of pistachios," she said, relieved.

"That's all?"

"Yes, and make sure it's Logan's chocolate, one-pound bar, and Lance Brothers pistachios."

"And this couldn't wait?"

"No, Luther, it cannot wait. I'm doing dessert for lunch tomorrow. If you don't want to go, then hush up and I'll go."

He slammed the door. His third step was into a shallow pothole. Cold water soaked his right ankle and oozed down quickly into his shoe. He froze for a second and caught his breath, then stepped away on his toes, trying desperately to spot other puddles while dodging traffic.

Chip's believed in high prices and modest rent. It was

on a side alley, not visible from anywhere really. Next to it was a wine shop run by a European of some strain who claimed to be French but was rumored to be Hungarian. His English was awful but he'd learned the language of price gouging. Probably learned it from Chip's next door. In fact all the shops in the District, as it was known, strove to be discriminating.

And every shop was full. Another Santa clanged away with the same bell outside the cheese shop. "Rudolph the Red-Nosed Reindeer" rattled from a hidden speaker above the sidewalk in front of Mother Earth, where the crunchy people were no doubt still wearing their sandals. Luther hated the store—refused to set foot inside. Nora bought organic herbs there, for what reason he'd never been certain. The old Mexican who owned the cigar store was happily stringing lights in his window, pipe stuck in the corner of his mouth, smoke drifting behind him, fake snow already sprayed on a fake tree.

There was a chance of real snow later in the night. The shoppers wasted no time as they hustled in and out of the stores. The sock on Luther's right foot was now frozen to his ankle.

There were no shopping baskets near the checkout at Chip's, and of course this was a bad sign. Luther didn't need one, but it meant the place was packed. The aisles were narrow and the inventory was laid out in such a way that nothing made sense. Regardless of what was on your list, you had to crisscross the place half a dozen times to finish up.

A stock boy was working hard on a display of Christmas chocolates. A sign by the butcher demanded that all good customers order their Christmas turkeys immediately. New Christmas wines were in! And Christmas hams!

What a waste, Luther thought to himself. Why do we eat so much and drink so much in the celebration of the birth of Christ? He found the pistachios near the bread. Odd how that made sense at Chip's. The white chocolate was nowhere near the baking section, so Luther cursed under his breath and trudged along the aisles, looking at everything. He got bumped by a shopping cart. No apology, no one noticed. "God Rest Ye Merry Gentlemen" was coming from above, as if Luther was supposed to be comforted. Might as well be "Frosty the Snowman."

Two aisles over, next to a selection of rice from around the world, there was a shelf of baking chocolates. As he stepped closer, he recognized a one-pound bar of Logan's. Another step closer and it suddenly disappeared, snatched from his grasp by a harsh-looking woman who never saw him. The little space reserved for Logan's was empty, and in the next desperate moment Luther saw not another speck of white chocolate. Lots of dark and medium chips and such, but nothing white.

The express line was, of course, slower than the other two. Chip's' outrageous prices forced its customers to buy in small quantities, but this had no effect whatsoever on the speed with which they came and went. Each item was lifted, inspected, and manually entered into the register by an unpleasant cashier. Sacking was hit or miss, though around Christmas the sackers came to life with smiles and enthusiasm and astounding recall of customers' names. It was the tipping season, yet another unseemly aspect of Christmas that Luther loathed.

Six bucks and change for a pound of pistachios. He shoved the eager young sacker away, and for a second thought he might have to strike him to keep his precious pistachios out of another bag. He stuffed them into the pocket of his overcoat and quickly left the store.

A crowd had stopped to watch the old Mexican decorate his cigar store window. He was plugging in little robots who trudged through the fake snow, and this delighted the crowd no end. Luther was forced to move off the curb, and in doing so he stepped just left instead of just right. His left foot sank into five inches of cold slush. He froze for a split second, sucking in lungfuls of cold air, cursing the old Mexican and his robots and his fans and the damned pistachios. He yanked his foot upward and slung dirty water on his pants leg, and standing at the curb with two frozen feet and the bell clanging away and "Santa Claus Is Coming to Town" blaring from the loudspeaker and the sidewalk blocked by revelers, Luther began to hate Christmas.

The water had seeped into his toes by the time he reached his car. "No white chocolate," he hissed at Nora as he crawled behind the wheel.

She was wiping her eyes.

"What is it now?" he demanded.

"I just talked to Blair."

"What? How? Is she all right?"

"She called from the airplane. She's fine." Nora was biting her lip, trying to recover.

Exactly how much does it cost to phone home from thirty thousand feet? Luther wondered. He'd seen phones on planes. Any credit card'll do. Blair had one he'd given her, the type where the bills are sent to Mom and Dad. From a cell phone up there to a cell phone down here, probably at least ten bucks.

And for what? I'm fine, Mom. Haven't seen you in almost an hour. We all love each other. We'll all miss each other. Gotta go, Mom.

The engine was running though Luther didn't remember starting it.

"You forgot the white chocolate?" Nora asked, fully recovered.

"No. I didn't forget it. They didn't have any."

"Did you ask Rex?"

"Who's Rex?"

"The butcher."

"No, Nora, for some reason I didn't think to ask the butcher if he had any white chocolate hidden among his chops and livers."

She yanked the door handle with all the frustration she could muster. "I have to have it. Thanks for nothing." And she was gone.

I hope you step in frozen water, Luther grumbled to himself. He fumed and muttered other unpleasantries. He switched the heater vents to the floorboard to thaw his feet, then watched the large people come and go at the burger place. Traffic was stalled on the streets beyond.

How nice it would be to avoid Christmas, he began to think. A snap of the fingers and it's January 2. No tree, no shopping, no meaningless gifts, no tipping, no clutter and wrappings, no traffic and crowds, no fruit-cakes, no liquor and hams that no one needed, no "Rudolph" and "Frosty," no office party, no wasted money. His list grew long. He huddled over the wheel, smiling now, waiting for heat down below, dreaming pleasantly of escape.

She was back, with a small brown sack which she tossed beside him just carefully enough not to crack the chocolate while letting him know that she'd found it and he hadn't. "Everybody knows you have to ask," she said sharply as she yanked at her shoulder harness.

"Odd way of marketing," Luther mused, in reverse now. "Hide it by the butcher, make it scarce, folks'll clamor for it. I'm sure they charge more if it's hidden."

"Oh hush, Luther."

"Are your feet wet?"

"No. Yours?"

"No."

"Then why'd you ask?"

"Just worried."

"Do you think she'll be all right?"

"She's on an airplane. You just talked to her."

"I mean down there, in the jungle."

"Stop worrying, okay? The Peace Corps wouldn't send her into a dangerous place."

"It won't be the same."

"What?"

"Christmas."

It certainly will not, Luther almost said. Oddly, he was smiling as he worked his way through traffic.

Two

....

$\mathcal{W}$ith his feet toasty and be-socked with heavy wool, Luther fell fast asleep and woke up even faster. Nora was roaming. She was in the bathroom flushing and flipping lights, then she left for the kitchen, where she fixed an herbal tea, then he heard her down the hall in Blair's room, no doubt staring at the walls and sniffling over where the years had gone. Then she was back in bed, rolling and jerking covers and trying her best to wake him. She wanted dialogue, a sounding board. She wanted Luther to assure her Blair was safe from the horrors of the Peruvian jungle.

But Luther was frozen, not flinching at any joint,

breathing as heavily as possible because if the dialogue began again it would run for hours. He pretended to snore and that settled her down.

It was after eleven when she grew still. Luther was wild-eyed, and his feet were smoldering. When he was absolutely certain she was asleep, he eased from the bed, ripped off the heavy socks and tossed them into a corner, and tiptoed down the hall to the kitchen for a glass of water. Then a pot of decaf.

An hour later he was in his basement office, at his desk with files open, the computer humming, spreadsheets in the printer, an investigator searching for evidence. Luther was a tax accountant by trade, so his records were meticulous. The evidence piled up and he forgot about sleep.

A year earlier, the Luther Krank family had spent $6,100 on Christmas—$6,100!—$6,100 on decorations, lights, flowers, a new Frosty, and a Canadian spruce; $6,100 on hams, turkeys, pecans, cheese balls, and cookies no one ate; $6,100 on wines and liquors and cigars around the office; $6,100 on fruitcakes from the firemen and the rescue squad, and calendars from the police association; $6,100 on Luther for a cashmere sweater he secretly loathed and a sports jacket he'd worn twice and an ostrich skin wallet that was quite expensive and quite ugly and frankly he didn't like the feel of. On Nora for a dress she wore to the company's Christmas dinner and her own cashmere sweater, which had not been seen since she unwrapped it, and a designer scarf she loved, $6,100. On Blair

$6,100 for an overcoat, gloves and boots, and a Walkman for her jogging, and, of course, the latest, slimmest cell phone on the market—$6,100 on lesser gifts for a select handful of distant relatives, most on Nora's side—$6,100 on Christmas cards from a stationer three doors down from Chip's, in the District, where all prices were double; $6,100 for the party, an annual Christmas Eve bash at the Krank home.

And what was left of it? Perhaps a useful item or two, but nothing much—$6,100!

With great relish Luther tallied the damage, as if it had been inflicted by someone else. All evidence was coming neatly together and making a very strong case.

He waffled a bit at the end, where he'd saved the charity numbers. Gifts to the church, to the toy drive, to the homeless shelter and the food bank. But he raced through the benevolence and came right back to the awful conclusion: $6,100 for Christmas.

"Nine percent of my adjusted gross," he said in disbelief. "Six thousand, one hundred. Cash. All but six hundred nondeductible."

In his distress, he did something he rarely did. Luther reached for the bottle of cognac in his desk drawer, and knocked back a few drinks.

He slept from three to six, and roared to life during his shower. Nora wanted to fret over coffee and oatmeal, but Luther would have none of it. He read the paper, laughed at the comics, assured her twice that Blair was having a ball, then kissed her and raced away to the office, a man on a mission.

The travel agency was in the atrium of Luther's building. He walked by it at least twice each day, seldom glancing at the window displays of beaches and mountains and sailboats and pyramids. It was there for those lucky enough to travel. Luther had never stepped inside, never thought about it actually. Their vacation was five days at the beach, in a friend's condo, and with his workload they were lucky to get that.

He stole away just after ten. He used the stairs so he wouldn't have to explain anything, and darted through the door of Regency Travel. Biff was waiting for him.

Biff had a large flower in her hair and a waxy bronze tan, and she looked as if she'd just dropped by the shop for a few hours between beaches. Her comely smile stopped Luther cold, and her first words left him flabbergasted. "You need a cruise," she said.

"How'd you know?" he managed to mumble. Her hand was out, grabbing his, shaking it, leading him to her long desk, where she placed him on one side while she perched herself on the other. Long bronze legs, Luther noted. Beach legs.

"December is the best time of year for a cruise," she began, and Luther was already sold. The brochures came in a torrent. She unfolded them across her desk, under his dreamy eyes.

"You work in the building?" she asked, easing near the issue of money.

"Wiley & Beck, sixth floor," Luther said without removing his eyes from the floating palaces, the endless beaches.

"Bail bondsmen?" she said.

Luther flinched just a bit. "No. Tax accountants."

"Sorry," she said, kicking herself. The pale skin, the dark eye circles, the standard blue oxford-cloth button-down with bad imitation prep school tie. She should have known better. Oh well. She reached for even glossier brochures. "Don't believe we get too many from your firm."

"We don't do vacations very well. Lots of work. I like this one right here."

"Great choice."

They settled on the *Island Princess,* a spanking-new mammoth vessel with rooms for three thousand, four pools, three casinos, nonstop food, eight stops in the Caribbean, and the list went on and on. Luther left with a stack of brochures and scurried back to his office six floors up.

The ambush was carefully planned. First, he worked late, which was certainly not unusual, but at any rate helped set the stage for the evening. He got lucky with the weather because it was still dreary. Hard to get in the spirit of the season when the skies were damp and gray. And much easier to dream about ten luxurious days in the sun.

If Nora wasn't worrying about Blair, then he'd certainly get her started. He'd simply mention some dreadful piece of news about a new virus or perhaps a Colombian village massacre, and that would set her off. Keep her mind off the joys of Christmas. Won't be the same without Blair, will it?

Why don't we take a break this year? Go hide. Go escape. Indulge ourselves.

Sure enough, Nora was off in the jungle. She hugged him and smiled and tried to hide the fact that she'd been crying. Her day had gone reasonably well. She'd survived the ladies' luncheon and spent two hours at the children's clinic, part of her grinding volunteer schedule.

While she heated up the pasta, he sneaked a reggae CD into the stereo, but didn't push Play. Timing was crucial.

They chatted about Blair, and not long into the dinner Nora kicked the door open. "It'll be so different this Christmas, won't it, Luther?"

"Yes it will," he said sadly, swallowing hard. "Nothing'll be the same."

"For the first time in twenty-three years, she won't be here."

"It might even be depressing. Lots of depression at Christmas, you know." Luther quickly swallowed and his fork grew still.

"I'd love to just forget about it," she said, her words ebbing at the end.

Luther flinched and cocked his good ear in her direction.

"What is it?" she asked.

"Well!!" he said dramatically, shoving his plate forward. "Now that you mention it. There's something I want to discuss with you."

"Finish your pasta."

"I'm finished," he announced, jumping to his feet. His briefcase was just a few steps away, and he attacked it.

"Luther, what are you doing?"

"Hang on."

He stood across the table from her, papers in both hands. "Here's my idea," he said proudly. "And it's brilliant."

"Why am I nervous?"

He unfolded a spreadsheet, and began pointing. "Here, my dear, is what we did last Christmas. Six thousand, one hundred dollars we spent on Christmas. Six thousand, one hundred dollars."

"I heard you the first time."

"And precious little to show for it. The vast majority of it down the drain. Wasted. And that, of course, does not include my time, your time, the traffic, stress, worry, bickering, ill-will, sleep loss—all the wonderful things that we pour into the holiday season."

"Where is this going?"

"Thanks for asking." Luther dropped the spreadsheets and, quick as a magician, presented the *Island Princess* to his wife. Brochures covered the table. "Where is this going, my dear? It's going to the Caribbean. Ten days of total luxury on the *Island Princess*, the fanciest cruise ship in the world. The Bahamas, Jamaica, Grand Cayman, oops, wait a minute."

Luther dashed into the den, hit the Play button, waited for the first notes, adjusted the volume, then dashed back to the kitchen where Nora was inspecting a brochure.

"What's that?" she asked.

"Reggae, the stuff they listen to down there. Anyway, where was I?"

"You were island hopping."

"Right, we'll snorkel on Grand Cayman, windsurf in Jamaica, lie on the beaches. Ten days, Nora, ten fabulous days."

"I'll have to lose some weight."

"We'll both go on a diet. Whatta you say?"

"What's the catch?"

"The catch is simple. We don't do Christmas. We save the money, spend it on ourselves for once. Not a dime on food we won't eat or clothes we won't wear or gifts no one needs. Not one red cent. It's a boycott, Nora, a complete boycott of Christmas."

"Sounds awful."

"No, it's wonderful. And it's just for one year. Let's take a break. Blair's not here. She'll be back next year and we can jump back into the Christmas chaos, if that's what you want. Come on, Nora, please. We skip Christmas, save the money, and go splash in the Caribbean for ten days."

"How much will it cost?"

"Three thousand bucks."

"So we save money?"

"Absolutely."

"When do we leave?"

"High noon, Christmas Day."

They stared at each other for a long time.

. . .

The deal was closed in bed, with the television on but muted, with magazines scattered over the sheets, all unread, with the brochures not far away on the night table. Luther was scanning a financial newspaper but seeing little. Nora had a paperback but the pages weren't turning.

The deal breaker had been their charitable giving. She simply refused to forgo it, or skip it, as Luther insisted on saying. She had reluctantly agreed to buy no gifts. She also wept at the thought of no tree, though Luther had mercilessly driven home the point that they yelled at each other every Christmas when they decorated the damned thing. And no Frosty on the roof ? When every house on the street would have one? Which brought up the issue of public ridicule. Wouldn't they be scorned for ignoring Christmas?

So what, Luther had replied over and over. Their friends and neighbors might disapprove at first, but secretly they would burn with envy. Ten days in the Caribbean, Nora, he kept telling her. Their friends and neighbors won't be laughing when they're shoveling snow, will they? No jeers from the spectators when we're roasting in the sun and they're bloated on turkey and dressing. No smirks when we return thin and tanned and completely unafraid of going to the mailbox.

Nora had seldom seen him so determined. He methodically killed all her arguments, one by one, until nothing was left but their charitable giving.

"You're going to let a lousy six hundred bucks stand between us and a Caribbean cruise?" Luther asked with great sarcasm.

"No, you are," she replied coolly.

And with that they went to their corners and tried to read.

But after a tense, silent hour, Luther kicked off the sheets and yanked off the wool socks and said, "All right. Let's match last year's charitable gifts, but not a penny more."

She flung her paperback and went for his neck. They embraced, kissed, then she reached for the brochures.

Three

....

*T*hough it was Luther's scheme, Nora was the first to be tested. The call came on Tuesday morning, from a pricklish man she didn't much care for. His name was Aubie, and he owned The Pumpkin Seed, a pompous little stationery store with a silly name and absurd prices.

After the obligatory greeting, Aubie came right to the point. "Just a bit worried about your Christmas cards, Mrs. Krank," he said, trying to seem deeply concerned.

"Why are you worried?" Nora asked. She did not like being hounded by a crabby shopkeeper who would barely speak to her the rest of the year.

"Oh well, you always select the most beautiful cards,

Mrs. Krank, and we need to order them now." He was bad at flattery. Every customer got the same line.

According to Luther's audit, The Pumpkin Seed had collected $318 from the Kranks last Christmas for cards, and at the moment it did seem somewhat extravagant. Not a major expense, but what did they get from it? Luther flatly refused to help with the addressing and stamping, and he flew hot every time she asked if so-and-so should be added to or deleted from their list. He also refused to offer so much as a glance at any of the cards they received, and Nora had to admit to herself that there was a diminishing joy in getting them.

So she stood straight and said, "We're not ordering cards this year." She could almost hear Luther applauding.

"Do what?"

"You heard me."

"May I ask why not?"

"You certainly may not."

To which Aubie had no response. He stuttered something then hung up, and for a moment Nora was filled with pride. She wavered, though, as she thought of the questions that would be raised. Her sister, their minister's wife, friends on the literacy board, her aunt in a retirement village—all would ask, at some point, what happened to their Christmas cards.

Lost in the mail? Ran out of time?

No. She would tell them the truth. No Christmas for us this year; Blair's gone and we're taking a cruise. And if you missed the cards that much, then I'll send you two next year.

Rallying, with a fresh cup of coffee, Nora asked herself how many of those on her list would even notice. She received a few dozen each year, a dwindling number, she admitted, and she kept no log of who bothered and who didn't. In the turmoil of Christmas, who really had time to fret over a card that didn't come?

Which brought up another of Luther's favorite holiday gripes—the emergency stash. Nora kept an extra supply so she could respond immediately to an unexpected card. Every year they received two or three from total strangers and a few from folks who hadn't sent them before, and within twenty-four hours she'd dash off the Kranks' holiday greetings in response, always with her standard handwritten note of good cheer and peace be with you.

Of course it was foolish.

She decided that she wouldn't miss the entire ritual of Christmas cards. She wouldn't miss the tedium of writing all those little messages, and hand-addressing a hundred or so envelopes, and stamping them, and mailing them, and worrying about who she forgot. She wouldn't miss the bulk they added to the daily mail, and the hastily opened envelopes, and the standard greetings from people as hurried as herself.

Freed of Christmas cards, Nora called Luther for a little propping. He was at his desk. She replayed the encounter with Aubie. "That little worm," Luther mumbled.

"Congratulations," he said when she finished.

"It wasn't hard at all," she gushed.

"Just think of all those beaches, dear, just waiting down there."

"What have you eaten?" she asked.

"Nothing. I'm still at three hundred calories."

"Me too."

When she hung up, Luther returned to the task at hand. He wasn't crunching numbers or grappling with IRS regs, as usual, but instead he was drafting a letter to his colleagues. His first Christmas letter. In it, he was carefully and artfully explaining to the office why he would not be participating in the holiday rituals, and, in turn, he would appreciate it if everyone else just left him alone. He would buy no gifts and would accept none. Thank you anyway. He would not attend the firm's black-tie Christmas dinner, nor would he be there for the drunken mess they called the office party. He didn't want the cognac and the ham that certain clients gave to all the big shots each year. He wasn't angry and he would not yell "Humbug!" at anyone who offered him a "Merry Christmas."

He was simply skipping Christmas. And taking a cruise instead.

He spent most of the quiet morning on his letter, and typed it himself. He would place a copy on every desk at Wiley & Beck.

• • •

The gravity of their scheme hit hard the next day, just after dinner. It was entirely possible to enjoy Christmas without cards, without parties and dinners, without needless gifts, without a lot of things that for some reason had been piled onto the birth of Christ. But how could anyone get through the holidays without a tree?

Skip the tree, and Luther knew they just might pull it off.

They were clearing the table, though there was precious little to clear. Baked chicken and cottage cheese made for an easy cleanup, and Luther was still hungry when the doorbell rang.

"I'll get it," he said. Through the front window of the living room he saw the trailer out in the street, and he knew instantly that the next fifteen minutes would not be pleasant. He opened the door and was met with three smiling faces—two youngsters dressed smartly in full Boy Scout regalia, and behind them Mr. Scanlon, the neighborhood's permanent scoutmaster. He too was in uniform.

"Good evening," Luther said to the kids.

"Hello, Mr. Krank. I'm Randy Bogan," said the taller of the two. "We're selling Christmas trees again this year."

"Got yours out on the trailer," said the shorter one.

"You had a Canadian blue spruce last year," Mr. Scanlon said.

Luther glanced beyond them, to the long flatbed trailer covered with two neat rows of trees. A small army of Scouts was busy unloading and hauling them away to Luther's neighbors.

"How much?" Luther asked.

"Ninety dollars," answered Randy. "We had to go up a little 'cause our supplier went up too."

Eighty last year, Luther almost said but held his tongue.

Nora materialized from nowhere and suddenly had her chin on his shoulder. "They're so cute," she whispered.

The boys or the trees? Luther almost asked. Why couldn't she stay in the kitchen and let him slug his way through this one?

With a big fake smile, Luther said, "Sorry, but we're not buying one this year."

Blank faces. Puzzled faces. Sad faces. A groan from just over his shoulder as the pain hit Nora. Looking at the boys, with his wife literally breathing down his neck, Luther Krank knew that this was the pivotal moment. Snap here, and the floodgates would open. Buy a tree, then decorate it, then realize that no tree looks complete without a pile of presents stuffed under it.

Hang tough, old boy, Luther urged himself, just as his wife whispered, "Oh dear."

"Hush," he hissed from the corner of his mouth.

The boys stared up at Mr. Krank, as if he'd just taken the last coins from their pockets.

"Sorry we had to go up on the price," Randy said sadly.

"We're making less per tree than last year," Mr. Scanlon added helpfully.

"It's not the price, boys," Luther said with another bogus grin. "We're not doing Christmas this year. Gonna be out of town. No need for a tree. Thanks anyway."

The boys began looking at their feet, as wounded children will do, and Mr. Scanlon appeared to be heartbroken. Nora offered another pitiful groan, and Luther, near panic, had a brilliant thought. "Don't you boys go out West each year, for a big camporee of some sort? New Mexico, in August, I seem to recall from a flyer."

They were caught off guard but all three nodded slowly.

"Good, here's the deal. I'll pass on the tree, but you guys come back in the summer and I'll give you a hundred bucks for your trip."

Randy Bogan managed to say "Thanks," but only because he felt obligated. They suddenly wanted to leave.

Luther slowly closed the door on them, then waited. They stood there on the front steps for a moment or two, then retreated down the drive, glancing over their shoulders.

When they reached the truck another adult, in uniform, was told the bizarre news. Others heard it, and before long activity around the trailer came to a halt as the Scouts and their leaders grouped at the end of the Kranks' driveway and stared at the Krank house as if aliens were on the roof.

Luther crouched low and peeked around the open curtains of the living room. "What are they doing?" Nora whispered behind him, crouching too.

"Just staring, I guess."

"Maybe we should've bought one."

"No."

"Don't have to put it up, you know."

"Quiet."

"Just keep it in the backyard."

"Stop it, Nora. Why are you whispering? This is our house."

"Same reason you're hiding behind the curtains."

He stood straight and closed the curtains. The Scouts moved on, their trailer inching down the street as the trees on Hemlock Street were delivered.

Luther built a fire and settled into his recliner for some reading, tax stuff. He was alone because Nora was pouting, a short spell that would be over by morning.

If he'd faced down the Boy Scouts, then who should he fear? More encounters were coming, no doubt, and that was one of the very reasons Luther disliked Christmas. Everybody selling something, raising money, looking for a tip, a bonus, something, something, something. He grew indignant again and felt fine.

He eased from the house an hour later. On the sidewalk that bordered Hemlock, he shuffled along, going nowhere. The air was cool and light. After a few steps he stopped by the Beckers' mailbox and looked into the front window of the living room, not far away. They were decorating their tree, and he could almost hear the bickering. Ned Becker was balancing himself on the top rung of a small ladder and stringing lights, while Jude Becker stood back a step and carped directions. Jude's mother, an ageless wonder even more terrifying than Jude herself, was also in on the fray. She was pointing directions to poor Ned, and her directions were in sharp conflict to those of Jude. String them here, string them there. That branch, no that other branch. Can't you see that gap there? What on earth are you looking at? Meanwhile, Rocky Becker, their twenty-year-old dropout, was sitting on the sofa with a can of something, laughing at them and offering advice that was apparently being ignored. He was the only one laughing, though.

The scene made Luther smile. It reinforced his wisdom, made him proud of his decision to simply avoid the whole mess.

He shuffled along, filling his haughty lungs with the cool air, happy that for the first time in his life he was eliminating the dreaded ritual of the tree trimming. Two doors down he stopped and watched the Frohmeyer clan assault an eight-foot spruce. Mr. Frohmeyer had brought two kids to the marriage. Mrs. Frohmeyer had arrived with three of her own, after which they produced another, making six, the eldest of which was no more than twelve. The entire brood was hanging ornaments and tinsel. At some point during every December Luther overheard one of the neighborhood women comment on just how awful the Frohmeyer tree looked. As if he cared.

Awful or not, they were certainly having a wonderful time draping it with tacky decorations. Frohmeyer did research at the university, $110,000 a year was the rumor, but with six kids there wasn't much to show for it. Their tree would be the last to come down after New Year's.

Luther turned around and headed home. At the Beckers', Ned was on the sofa with an icepack on his shoulder, Jude hovering over him, lecturing with her finger. The ladder was on its side, being inspected by the mother-in-law. Whatever the cause of the fall, there was no doubt that all blame would be placed on poor Ned.

Great, thought Luther. Now I'll have to listen to details of another ailment for the next four months. Come to think of it, Ned Becker had fallen off that ladder before, five maybe six years earlier. Crashed into the tree and knocked the whole thing over. Broke Jude's keepsake ornaments. She'd pouted for a year.

What madness, thought Luther.

Four

....

$\mathcal{N}$ora and two friends had just captured a table at their favorite deli, a converted service station that still sold gas but had also added designer sandwiches and latte at three bucks a cup. As always, it was packed at noon, and the long lines attracted even more folks.

It was a working lunch. Candi and Merry were the other two members of a committee to oversee an auction for the art museum. Around most of the other tables, similar fund-raisers were being plotted with great effort.

Nora's cell phone rang. She apologized because she had forgotten to turn it off, but Merry insisted she take the call anyway. Cell phones were buzzing all over the deli.

It was Aubie again, and at first she was puzzled as to how he had obtained her number. But then, she routinely gave it away.

"It's Aubie from The Pumpkin Seed," she explained to Candi and Merry, thereby linking them to the conversation. They nodded with disinterest. Presumably, everybody knew Aubie from The Pumpkin Seed. He had the highest prices in the world so if you shopped there you could one-up anyone when it came to stationery.

"We forgot to discuss your party invitations," Aubie said, and Nora's heart froze. She, too, had forgotten the invitations, and she certainly didn't want to discuss them in front of Merry and Candi.

"Oh yes," she said. Merry had struck up a conversation with a volunteer at the next table. Candi was scanning the deli to see who wasn't there.

"We won't be needing them, either," Nora said.

"No party?" Aubie asked, his words laden with curiosity.

"Yes, no party this year."

"Well, I—"

"Thanks for calling, Aubie," she said softly and quickly and snapped the phone shut.

"Won't be needing what?" Merry asked, suddenly breaking off her other conversation and honing in on Nora.

"No party this year?" Candi asked, her eyes locking on to Nora's like radar. "What's up?"

Grit your teeth, Nora urged herself. Think of beaches, warm salt water, ten days in paradise. "Oh that," she said. "We're taking a cruise this year instead of doing Christmas. Blair's gone, you know, we need a break."

The deli was suddenly quiet, or at least it seemed so to Nora. Candi and Merry frowned as they replayed this news. Nora, with Luther's words ringing in her ears, pushed the offensive. "Ten days on the *Island Princess,* a luxury liner. Bahamas, Jamaica, Grand Cayman. I've already lost two pounds," she said with a cheerful smugness.

"You're not doing Christmas?" Merry said in disbelief.

"That's what I said," Nora responded. Merry was quick with a judgment, and years ago Nora had learned to bite back. She stiffened, ready for a sharp word.

"How do you simply not do Christmas?" Merry asked.

"You skip it," Nora replied, as if that would explain everything.

"Sounds wonderful," Candi said.

"Then what do we do Christmas Eve?" Merry asked.

"You'll think of something," Nora replied. "There are other parties."

"But none like yours."

"You're sweet."

"When do you leave?" Candi asked, dreaming now of beaches and no in-laws piled in for a week.

"Christmas Day. Around noon." It was an odd time to leave, she had thought after Luther had booked the cruise. If we're not celebrating Christmas, dear, she'd said, why not leave a few days earlier? Avoid Christmas Eve while we're at it. Eliminate the whole crazy mess. "What if Blair calls Christmas Eve?" he'd replied. And besides, Biff got $399 knocked off the package because few people travel on the twenty-fifth. Anyway, it was booked and paid for and nothing was going to change.

"Then why not have the party on Christmas Eve anyway?" Merry asked, getting pushy, fearful that she might feel obligated to host a replacement.

"Because we don't want to, Merry. We're taking a break, okay. A year off. No Christmas whatsoever. Nothing. No tree, no turkey, no gifts. We're taking the money and splurging on a cruise. Get it?"

"I get it," Candi said. "I wish Norman would do something like that. He wouldn't dream of it, though, afraid he'd miss twenty or so bowl games. I'm so envious, Nora."

And with that Merry took a bite of her avocado sandwich. She chewed and began glancing around the deli. Nora knew exactly what she was thinking. Who can I tell first? The Kranks are skipping Christmas! No party! No tree! Nothing but money in their pockets so they can blow it on a cruise.

Nora ate too, knowing that as soon as she stepped through the door over there the gossip would roar through the deli and before dinner everyone in her world would know the news. So what? she told herself. It was inevitable, and why was it such a big deal? Half would be in Candi's camp, burning with envy and dreaming along with Nora. Half would be with Merry, seemingly appalled at the notion of simply eliminating Christmas, but even within this group of critics Nora suspected many would secretly covet their cruise.

And in three months who'd care anyway?

After a few bites they shoved their sandwiches aside and brought out the paperwork. Not another word was mentioned about Christmas, not in Nora's presence anyway. Driving away, she phoned Luther with the news of their latest victory.

Luther was up and down. His secretary, a fifty-year-old triple divorcée named Dox, had quipped that she'd have to buy her own cheap perfume, she supposed, since Santa wasn't coming this year. He'd been called Scrooge twice, and each time the name had been followed by a fit of laughter. How original, Luther thought.

Late in the morning, Yank Slader darted into Luther's office as if angry clients were chasing him. Peeking out first, he closed the door, then assumed a seat. "You're a genius, old boy," he said almost in a whisper. Yank was an amortization specialist, afraid of his shadow, loved eighteen-hour days because his wife was a brawler.

"Of course I am," said Luther.

"Went home last night, late, got the wife to bed then did the same thing you did. Crunched the numbers, went through the bank statements, the works, came up with almost seven grand. What was your damage?"

"Just over six thousand."

"Unbelievable, and not a rotten thing to show for it. Makes me sick."

"Take a cruise," Luther said, knowing full well that Yank's wife would never agree to such foolishness. For her, the holidays began in late October and steadily gathered momentum until the big bang, a ten-hour marathon on Christmas Day with four meals and a packed house.

"Take a cruise," Yank mumbled. "Can't think of anything worse. Socked away on a boat with Abigail for ten days. I'd pitch her overboard."

And no one would blame you, Luther thought.

"Seven thousand bucks," Yank repeated to himself.

"Ridiculous, isn't it?" Luther said, and for a moment both accountants silently lamented the waste of hard-earned money.

"Your first cruise?" Yank asked.

"Yes."

"Never done one myself. Wonder if they have single folks on board?"

"I'm sure they do. There's no requirement you have to take a partner. Thinking of going solo, Yank?"

"Not thinking, Luther, dreaming." He drifted off, his hollow eyes showing a hint of hope, of fun, of something Luther had never seen before in Yank. He left the room there for a moment, his thoughts running wildly across the Caribbean, so wonderfully alone without Abigail.

Luther was quiet while his colleague dreamed, but the dreams soon became slightly embarrassing. Fortunately, the phone rang and Yank was jolted back to a harsh world of amortization tables and a quarrelsome wife. He got to his feet and seemed to be leaving without a word. At the door, though, he said, "You're my hero, Luther."

. . .

Vic Frohmeyer had heard the rumor from Mr. Scanlon, the scoutmaster, and from his wife's niece, who roomed with a girl who worked part time for Aubie at The Pumpkin Seed, and from a colleague at the university whose brother got his taxes done by someone at Wiley & Beck. Three different sources, and the rumor had to be true. Krank could do whatever he damned well pleased, but Vic and the rest of Hemlock wouldn't take it lying down.

Frohmeyer was the unelected ward boss of Hemlock. His cushy job at the university gave him time to meddle, and his boundless energy kept him on the street organizing all sorts of activities. With six kids, his house was the undisputed hangout. The doors were always open, a game always in progress. As a result, his lawn had a worn look to it, though he worked hard in his flower beds.

It was Frohmeyer who brought the candidates to Hemlock for barbecues in his backyard, and for their campaign pledges. It was Frohmeyer who circulated the petitions, knocking door to door, gathering momentum against annexation or in favor of school bonds or against a new four-lane miles away or in favor of a new sewer system. It was Frohmeyer who called Sanitation when a neighbor's garbage was not picked up, and because it was Frohmeyer the matter got quickly resolved. A stray dog, one from another street, a call from Vic Frohmeyer, and Animal Control was on the spot. A stray kid, one with hair and tattoos and the leery look of a delinquent, and Frohmeyer would have the police poking him in the chest and asking questions.

A hospital stay on Hemlock, and the Frohmeyers arranged visitation and food and even lawn care. A death on Hemlock, and they organized flowers for the funeral and visits to the cemetery. A neighbor in need could call the Frohmeyers for anything.

The Frostys had been Vic's idea, though he'd seen it in a suburb of Evanston and thus couldn't take full credit. The same Frosty on every Hemlock roof, an eight-foot

Frosty with a goofy smile around a corncob pipe and a black top hat and thick rolls around the middle, all made to glow a brilliant white by a two-hundred-watt bulb screwed into a cavity somewhere near Frosty's colon. The Hemlock Frostys had made their debut six years earlier and were a smashing success—twenty-one houses on one side, twenty-one on the other, the street lined with two perfect rows of Frostys, forty feet up. A color photo with a cute story ran on the front page. Two television news crews had done Live! reports.

The next year, Stanton Street to the south and Acker-man Street to the north had jumped in with Rudolphs and silver bells, respectively, and a committee from Parks and Rec, at Frohmeyer's quiet urging, began giving neighbor-hood awards for Christmas decorations.

Two years earlier disaster struck when a windstorm sent most of the Frostys airborne into the next precinct. Frohmeyer rallied the neighbors though, and last year a new, slightly shorter version of Frosty decorated Hemlock. Only two houses had not participated.

Each year, Frohmeyer decided the date on which to resurrect the Frostys, and after hearing the rumors about Krank and his cruise he decided to do it immediately. After dinner, he typed a short memo to his neighbors, something he did at least twice a month, ran forty-one copies, and dis-patched his six children to hand-deliver them to every house on Hemlock. It read: "Neighbor—Weather tomorrow should be clear, an excellent time to bring Frosty back to life—Call Marty or Judd or myself if you need assistance—Vic Frohmeyer."

Luther took the memo from a smiling kid.

"Who is it?" Nora called from the kitchen.

"Frohmeyer."

"What's it about?"

"Frosty."

She walked slowly into the living room, where Luther was holding the half-sheet of paper as if it were a summons to jury duty. They gave each other a fearful look, and very slowly Luther began shaking his head.

"You have to do it," she said.

"No, I do not," he said, very firmly, his temper rising with each word. "I certainly do not. I will not be told by Vic Frohmeyer that I have to decorate my house for Christmas."

"It's just Frosty."

"No, it is much more."

"What?"

"It's the principle of it, Nora. Don't you understand? We can forget about Christmas if we damned well choose, and—"

"Don't swear, Luther."

"And no one, not even Vic Frohmeyer, can stop us." Louder. "I will not be forced into doing this!" He was pointing to the ceiling with one hand and waving the memo with the other. Nora retreated to the kitchen.

Five

....

A Hemlock Frosty came in four sections—a wide round base, a slightly smaller snowball that wedged into the base, then a trunk, then the head with the face and hat. Each section could be stuffed into the next larger one, so that storage for the other eleven months of the year was not too demanding. At a cost of $82.99, plus shipping, everyone packed away their Frostys with care.

And they unpacked them with great delight. Throughout the afternoon sections of Frostys could be seen inside most garages along Hemlock as the snowmen were dusted off and checked for parts. Then they were put together, built just like a real snowman, section on top of section, until they were seven feet tall and ready for the roof.

Installation was not a simple matter. A ladder and a rope were required, along with the help of a neighbor. First, the roof had to be scaled with a rope around the waist, then Frosty, who was made of hard plastic and weighed about forty pounds, was hoisted up, very carefully so as not to scratch him over the asphalt shingles. When Frosty reached the summit, he was strapped to the chimney with a canvas band that Vic Frohmeyer had invented himself. A two-hundred-watt lamp was screwed into Frosty's innards, and an extension cord was dropped from the backside of the roof.

Wes Trogdon was an insurance broker who'd called in sick so he could surprise his kids by having their Frosty up first. He and his wife, Trish, washed their snowman just after lunch, then, under her close supervision, Wes climbed and grappled and adjusted until the task was complete. Forty feet high, with a splendid view, he looked up and down Hemlock and was quite smug that he had got the jump on everyone, including Frohmeyer.

While Trish made hot cocoa, Wes began hauling boxes of lights up from the basement to the driveway, where he laid them out and checked circuits. No one on Hemlock strung more Christmas lights than the Trogdons. They lined their yard, wrapped their shrubs, draped their trees, outlined their house, adorned their windows—fourteen thousand lights the year before.

Frohmeyer left work early so he could supervise matters on Hemlock, and he was quite pleased to see activity. He was momentarily jealous that Trogdon had beaten him to the punch, but what did it really matter? Before long they joined forces in the driveway of Mrs. Ellen Mulholland, a lovely widow who was already baking brownies. Her Frosty was up in a flash, her brownies devoured, and they were off to render more assistance. Kids joined them, including Spike Frohmeyer, a twelve-year-old with his father's flair for organization and community activism, and they went door to door in the late afternoon, hurrying before darkness slowed them.

At the Kranks', Spike rang the doorbell but got no response. Mr. Krank's Lexus was not there, which was certainly not unusual at 5 P.M. But Mrs. Krank's Audi was in the garage, a sure sign that she was home. The curtains and shades were pulled. No answer at the door though, and the gang moved to the Beckers', where Ned was in the front yard washing his Frosty with his mother-in-law barking instructions from the steps.

"They're leaving now," Nora whispered into the phone in their bedroom.

"Why are you whispering?" Luther asked with agitation.

"Because I don't want them to hear me."

"Who is it?"

"Vic Frohmeyer, Wes Trogdon, looks like that Brixley fellow from the other end of the street, some kids."

"A regular bunch of thugs, huh?"

"More like a street gang. They're at the Beckers' now."

"God help them."

"Where's Frosty?" she asked.

"Same place he's been since January. Why?"

"Oh, I don't know."

"This is comical, Nora. You're whispering into the phone, in a locked house, because our neighbors are going door to door helping our other neighbors put up a ridiculous seven-foot plastic snowman, which, by the way, has absolutely nothing to do with Christmas. Ever think about that, Nora?"

"No."

"We voted for Rudolph, remember?"

"No."

"It's comical."

"I'm not laughing."

"Frosty's taking a year off, okay? The answer is no."

Luther hung up gently and tried to concentrate on his work. After dark, he drove home, slowly, all the way telling himself that it was silly to be worried about such trivial matters as putting a snowman on the roof. And all the way he kept thinking of Walt Scheel.

"Come on, Scheel," he mumbled to himself. "Don't let me down."

Walt Scheel was his rival on Hemlock, a grumpy sort who lived directly across the street. Two kids out of college, a wife battling breast cancer, a mysterious job with a Belgian conglom, an income that appeared to be in the upper range on Hemlock—but regardless of what he earned Scheel and the missus expected their neighbors to think they had a lot more. Luther bought a Lexus, Scheel had to have one. Bellington put in a pool, Scheel suddenly needed to swim in his own backyard, doctor's orders. Sue Kropp on the west end outfitted her kitchen with designer appliances—$8,000 was the rumor—and Bev Scheel spent $9,000 six months later.

A hopeless cook, Bev's cuisine tasted worse after the renovation, according to witnesses.

Their haughtiness had been stopped cold, however, with the breast cancer eighteen months earlier. The Scheels had been humbled mightily. Keeping ahead of the neighbors didn't matter anymore. Things were useless. They had endured the disease with a quiet dignity, and, as usual, Hemlock had supported them like family. A year after the first chemo, the Belgian conglom had reshuffled itself. Whatever Walt's job had been, it was now something less.

The Christmas before the Scheels had been too distracted to decorate. No Frosty for them, not much of a tree, just a few lights strung around the front window, almost an afterthought.

A year earlier, two houses on Hemlock had gone without Frostys—the Scheels' and one on the west end owned by a Pakistani couple who'd lived there three months then moved away. It had been for sale, and Frohmeyer had actually considered ordering another Frosty and conducting a nighttime raid on the premises to erect it.

"Come on, Scheel," Luther mumbled in traffic. "Keep your Frosty in the basement."

The Frosty idea had been cute six years earlier when first hatched by Frohmeyer. Now it was tedious. But, Luther confessed, certainly not tedious to the kids on Hemlock. He had been secretly delighted two years before when the storm gusts cleared the roofs and sent Frostys flying over half the city.

He turned onto Hemlock, and as far as he could see the street was lined with identical snowmen sitting like glowing sentries above the houses. Just two gaps in their ranks—the Scheels and the Kranks. "Thank you, Scheel," Luther whispered. Kids were riding bikes. Neighbors were outside, stringing lights, chatting across hedgerows.

A street gang was meeting in Scheel's garage, Luther noticed as he parked and walked hurriedly into his house. Sure enough, within minutes a ladder went up and Frohmeyer scurried up like a veteran roofer. Luther peeked through the blinds on his front door. There was Walt Scheel standing in the front yard with a dozen people, Bev, bundled up in a warm coat, on the front steps. Spike Frohmeyer was wrestling with an extension cord. There were shouts and laughter, everyone seemed to be hurling instructions to Frohmeyer as the next to the last Frosty on Hemlock was heaved up.

Little was said over a dinner of sauceless pasta and cottage cheese. Nora was down three pounds, Luther four. After the dishes, he went to the treadmill in the basement where he walked for fifty minutes, burning 340 calories, more than he had just consumed. He took a shower and tried to read.

When the street was clear, he went for a walk. He would not be a prisoner in his home. He would not hide from his neighbors. He had nothing to fear from these people.

There was a twinge of guilt as he admired the two

neat lines of snowmen guarding their quiet street. The Trogdons were piling more ornaments on their tree, and it brought back a few distant memories of Blair's childhood and those faraway times. He was not the nostalgic type. You live life today, not tomorrow, certainly not yesterday, he always said. The warm memories were quickly erased with thoughts of shopping and traffic and burning money. Luther was quite proud of his decision to take a year off.

His belt was a bit looser. The beaches were waiting.

A bike rushed in from nowhere and slid to a stop. "Hi, Mr. Krank."

It was Spike Frohmeyer, no doubt heading home after some clandestine juvenile meeting. The kid slept less than his father, and the neighborhood was full of stories about Spike's nocturnal ramblings. He was a nice boy, but usually unmedicated.

"Hello, Spike," Luther said, catching his breath. "What brings you out?"

"Just checking on things," he said, as if he were the official night watchman.

"What kind of things, Spike?"

"My dad sent me over to Stanton Street to see how many Rudolphs are up."

"How many?" Luther asked, playing along.

"None. We smoked 'em again."

What a victorious night the Frohmeyers would have, Luther thought. Silly.

"You putting yours up, Mr. Krank?"

"No, I'm not, Spike. We're leaving town this year, no Christmas for us."

"I didn't know you could do that."

"This is a free country, Spike, you can do almost anything you want."

"You're not leaving till Christmas Day," Spike said.

"What?"

"Noon's what I heard. You got plenty of time to get Frosty up. That way we can win the award again."

Luther paused for a second and once more marveled at the speed with which one person's private business could be so thoroughly kicked around the neighborhood.

"Winning is overrated, Spike," he said wisely. "Let another street have the award this year."

"I guess so."

"Now run along."

He rolled away and said, "See you later," over his shoulder.

The kid's father was lying in ambush when Luther came strolling by. "Evening, Luther," Vic said, as if the encounter was purely by chance. He leaned on his mailbox at the end of his drive.

"Evening, Vic," Luther said, almost stopping. But at the last second he decided to keep walking. He stepped around Frohmeyer, who tagged along.

"How's Blair?"

"Fine, Vic, thanks. How are your kids?"

"In great spirits. It's the best time of the year, Luther. Don't you think so?" Frohmeyer had picked up the pace and the two were now side by side.

"Absolutely. I couldn't be happier. Do miss Blair, though. It won't be the same without her."

"Of course not."

They stopped in front of the Beckers', next door to Luther's, and watched as poor Ned teetered on the top step of the ladder in a vain effort to mount an oversized star on the highest branch of the tree. His wife stood behind him, helping mightily with her instructions but not once holding the ladder, and his mother-in-law was a few steps back for the wide view. A fistfight seemed imminent.

"Some things about Christmas I'm not going to miss," Luther said.

"So you're really skipping out?"

"You got it, Vic. I'd appreciate your cooperation."

"Just doesn't seem right for some reason."

"That's not for you to decide, is it?"

"No, it's not."

"Good night, Vic." Luther left him there, amused by the Beckers.

Six

....

$\mathcal{N}$ora's late-morning round-table at the shelter for battered women ended badly when Claudia, a casual friend at best, blurted out randomly, "So, Nora, no Christmas Eve bash this year?"

Of the eight women present, including Nora, exactly five had been invited to her Christmas parties in the past. Three had not, and at the moment those three looked for a hole to crawl into, as did Nora.

You crude little snot, thought Nora, but she managed to say quickly, "Afraid not. We're taking a year off." To which she wanted to add, "And if we ever have another party, Claudia dear, don't hold your breath waiting for an invitation."

"I heard you're taking a cruise," said Jayne, one of the three excluded, trying to reroute the conversation.

"We are, leaving Christmas Day in fact."

"So you're just eliminating Christmas altogether?" asked Beth, another casual acquaintance who got invited each year only because her husband's firm did business with Wiley & Beck.

"Everything," Nora said aggressively as her stomach tightened.

"That's a good way to save money," said Lila, the biggest bitch of the bunch. Her emphasis on the word "money" implied that perhaps things were a bit tight around the Krank household. Nora's cheeks began to burn. Lila's husband was a pediatrician. Luther knew for a fact that they were heavily in debt—big house, big cars, country clubs. Earned a lot, spent even more.

Thinking of Luther, where was he in these awful moments? Why was she taking the brunt of his harebrained scheme? Why was she on the front lines while he sat smugly in his quiet office dealing with people who either worked for him or were afraid of him? It was a good-old-boy club, Wiley & Beck, a bunch of stuffy tight-fisted accountants who were probably toasting Luther for his bravery in avoiding Christmas and saving a few bucks. If his defiance could become a trend anywhere, it was certainly in the accounting profession.

Here she was getting scorched again while Luther was safely at work, probably playing the hero.

Women handled Christmas, not men. They shopped and decorated and cooked, planned parties and sent cards and fretted over things the men never thought about. Why, exactly, was Luther so keen on dodging Christmas when he put so little effort into it?

Nora fumed but held her fire. No sense starting an all-girl rumble at the center for battered women.

Someone mentioned adjournment and Nora was the first out of the room. She fumed even more as she drove home—unpleasant thoughts about Lila and her comment about money. Even uglier thoughts about her husband and his selfishness. She was sorely tempted to cave right then, go on a spree and have the house decorated by the time he got home. She could have a tree up in two hours. It wasn't too late to plan her party. Frohmeyer would be happy to take care of their Frosty. Cut back on the gifts and a few other things, and they would still save enough to pay for the cruise.

She turned onto Hemlock and of course the first thing she noticed was the fact that only one house had no snowman on the roof. Leave it to Luther. Their pretty two-story brick home standing alone, as if the Kranks were Hindus or Buddhists, some strain that didn't believe in Christmas.

She stood in her living room and looked out the front window, directly through the spot where their beautiful tree always stood, and for the first time Nora was struck with how cold and undecorated her house was. She bit her lip and went for the phone, but Luther had stepped out for a sandwich. In the stack of mail she'd retrieved from the box, between two envelopes containing holiday cards, she saw something that stopped her cold. Airmail, from Peru. Spanish words stamped on the front.

Nora sat down and tore it open. It was two pages of Blair's lovely handwriting, and the words were precious.

She was having a great time in the wilds of Peru. Couldn't be better, living with an Indian tribe that had been around for several thousand years. They were very poor, according to our standards, but healthy and happy. The children were at first very distant, but they had come around, wanting to learn. Blair rambled on a bit about the children.

She was living in a grass hut with Stacy, her new friend from Utah. Two other Peace Corps volunteers lived nearby. The corps had started the small school four years earlier. Anyway, she was healthy and well fed, no dreaded diseases or deadly animals had been spotted, and the work was challenging.

The last paragraph was the jolt of fortitude that Nora so desperately needed. It read:

> I know it will be difficult not having me there for Christmas, but please don't be sad. My children know nothing of Christmas. They have so little, and want so little, it makes me feel guilty for the mindless materialism of our culture. There are no calendars here, and no clocks, so I doubt if I'll even know when it comes and goes.
>
> (Besides, we can catch up next year, can't we?)

Such a smart girl. Nora read it again and was suddenly filled with pride, not only for raising such a wise and mature daughter but also for her own decision to forgo, at least for a year, the mindless materialism of our culture.

She called Luther again and read him the letter.

. . .

Monday night at the mall! Not Luther's favorite place, but he sensed Nora needed a night out. They had dinner in a fake pub on one end, then fought through the masses to get to the other, where a star-filled romantic comedy was opening at the multiplex. Eight bucks a ticket, for what Luther knew would be another dull two hours of overpaid clowns giggling their way through a subliterate plot. But anyway, Nora loved the movies and he tagged along to keep peace. Despite the crowds, the cinema was deserted, and this thrilled Luther when he realized that everybody else was out there shopping. He settled low in his seat with his popcorn, and went to sleep.

He awoke with an elbow in his ribs. "You're snoring," Nora hissed at him.

"Who cares? The place is empty."

"Hush up, Luther."

He watched the movie, but after five minutes had had enough. "I'll be back," he whispered, and left. He'd rather fight through the mob and get stepped on than watch such foolishness. He rode the escalator to the upper level, where he leaned on the rail and watched the chaos below. A Santa was holding court on his throne and the line was moving very slowly. Over at the ice rink the music blared from scratchy speakers while kids in elf costumes skated around some stuffed creature that appeared to be a reindeer. Every parent watched through the lens of a videocamera. Weary shoppers trudged along, lugging shopping bags, bumping into others, fighting with their children.

Luther had never felt prouder.

Across the way, he saw a new sporting goods store. He strolled over, noticing through the window that there was a crowd inside and certainly not enough cashiers. He was just browsing, though. He found the snorkel gear in the back, a rather slim selection, but it was December. The swimsuits were of the Speedo variety, breathtakingly narrow all the way around and designed solely for Olympic swimmers under the age of twenty. More of a pouch than a garment. He was afraid to touch them. He'd get himself a catalog and shop from the safety of his home.

As he left the store an argument was raging at a checkout, something about a layaway that got lost. What fools.

He bought himself a fat-free yogurt and killed time strolling along the upper concourse, smiling smugly at the harried souls burning their way through their paychecks. He stopped and gawked at a life-sized poster of a gorgeous young thing in a string bikini, her skin perfectly tanned. She was inviting him to step inside a small salon called Tans Forever. Luther glanced around as if it were an adult bookstore, then ducked inside where Daisy was waiting behind a magazine. Her brown face forced a smile and seemed to crack along the forehead and around the eyes. Her teeth had been whitened, her hair lightened, her skin darkened, and for a second Luther wondered what she looked like before the project.

Not surprisingly, Daisy said it was the best time of the year to purchase a package. Their Christmas special was twelve sessions for $60. Only one session every other day, fifteen minutes at first, but working up to a max of twenty-five. When the package was over, Luther would be superbly tanned and certainly prepared for anything the Caribbean sun could throw at him.

He followed her a few steps to a row of booths—flimsy little rooms with a tanning bed each and not much else. They were now featuring state-of-the-art FX-2000 BronzeMats, straight from Sweden, as if the Swedes knew everything about sunbathing. At first glance, the Bronze-Mat horrified Luther. Daisy explained that you simply undressed, yes, everything, she purred, slid into the unit, and pulled the top down in a manner that reminded Luther of a waffle iron. Cook for fifteen or twenty minutes, a timer goes off, get up, get dressed. Nothing to it.

"How much do you sweat?" Luther asked, struggling with the image of himself lying completely exposed while eighty lamps baked all parts of his body.

She explained that things got warm. Once done, you simply wiped off your BronzeMat with a spray and paper towels, and things were suitable for the next guy.

Skin cancer? he inquired. She offered a phony laugh. No way. Perhaps with the older units before they perfected the technology to virtually eliminate ultraviolet rays and such. The new BronzeMats were actually safer than the sun itself. She'd been tanning for eleven years.

And your skin looks like burnt cowhide, Luther mused to himself.

He signed up for two packages for $120. He left the salon with the determination to get himself tanned, however uncomfortable it would be. And he chuckled at the thought of Nora stripping down behind paper-thin walls and inserting herself into the BronzeMat.

Seven

....

$\mathscr{T}$he officer's name was
Salino, and he came around every year. He was portly, wore
no gun or vest, no Mace or nightstick, no flashlight or silver
bullets, no handcuffs or radio, none of the mandatory gad-
getry that his brethren loved to affix to their belts and bodies. Salino looked bad in his uniform, but he'd been looking
bad for so long that no one cared. He patrolled the south-
east, the neighborhoods around Hemlock, the affluent suburbs where the only crime was an occasional stolen bike or
a speeding car.

Salino's partner for the evening was a beefy, lockjawed
young lad with a roll of muscle bulging from the collar of

his navy shirt. Treen was his name, and Treen wore every device and doohickey that Salino did not.

When Luther saw them through the blinds on his front door, standing there pressing his doorbell, he instantly thought of Frohmeyer. Frohmeyer could summon the police to Hemlock faster than the Chief himself.

He opened the door, made the obligatory hellos and good evenings, then asked them to step inside. He didn't want them inside, but he knew they would not leave until they completed the ritual. Treen was grasping a plain white tube that held the calendar.

Nora, who just seconds ago had been watching television with her husband, had suddenly vanished, though Luther knew she was just beyond the French doors, hiding in the kitchen, missing not a word.

Salino did all the talking. Luther figured this was because his hulking partner probably possessed a limited vocabulary. The Police Benevolent Association was once again working at full throttle to do all sorts of wonderful things for the community. Toys for tots. Christmas baskets for the less fortunate. Visits by Santa. Ice skating adventures. Trips to the zoo. And they were delivering gifts to the old folks in the nursing homes and to the veterans tucked away in wards. Salino had perfected his presentation. Luther had heard it before.

To help defray the costs of their worthy projects this year, the Police Benevolent Association had once again put together a handsome calendar for next year, one that again featured some of its members in action shots as they served the people. Treen on cue whipped out Luther's calendar, un-rolled it, and flipped the rather large sheets as Salino did the play by play. For January it was a traffic cop with a warm smile waving little kindergartners across the street. For February, it was a cop even beefier than Treen helping a stranded motorist change a tire. Somehow in the midst of the effort the policeman had managed a smile. For March it was a rather tense scene at a nighttime accident with lights flashing all around and three men in blue conferring with frowns.

Luther admired the photos and artwork without a word as the months marched along.

What about the leopard print briefs? he wanted to ask. Or the steam room? Or the lifeguard with just a towel around his waist? Three years earlier, the PBA had suc-cumbed to trendier tastes and published a calendar filled with photos of its leaner and younger members, all clad in virtually nothing, half grinning goofily at the camera, the other half straining with the tortured I-hate-modeling ve-neer of contemporary fashion. Practically R-rated, a big story about it made the front page.

Quite a brouhaha erupted overnight. The Mayor was incensed as complaints flooded city hall. The director of the PBA got fired. The undistributed calendars were pulled and burned while the local TV station recorded it Live!

Nora kept theirs in the basement, where she secretly enjoyed it all year.

The beefcake calendar was a financial disaster for all concerned, but it created more interest the following Christmas. Sales almost doubled.

Luther bought one every year, but only because it was expected. Oddly, there was no price attached to the calendars, at least not to the ones delivered personally by the likes of Salino and Treen. Their personal touch cost something more, an additional layer of goodwill that people like Luther were expected to fork over simply because that was the way it was done. It was this coerced, above-the-table bribery that Luther hated. Last year he'd written a check for a hundred bucks to the PBA, but not this year.

When the presentation was over, Luther stood tall and said, "I don't need one." Salino cocked his head to one side as if he'd misunderstood. Treen's neck puffed out another inch.

Salino's face turned into a smirk. You may not need one, the smirk said, but you'll buy it anyway. "Why's that?" he said.

"I already have calendars for next year." That was news to Nora, who was biting a fingernail and holding her breath.

"But not like this," Treen managed to grunt. Salino shot him a look that said, "Be quiet!"

"I have two calendars in my office and two on my desk," Luther said. "We have one by the phone in the kitchen. My watch tells me precisely what day it is, as does my computer. Haven't missed a day in years."

"We're raising money for crippled children, Mr. Krank," Salino said, his voice suddenly soft and scratchy. Nora felt a tear coming.

"We give to crippled children, Officer," Luther shot

back. "Through the United Way and our church and our taxes we give to every needy group you can possibly name."

"You're not proud of your policemen?" Treen said roughly, no doubt repeating a line he'd heard Salino use on others.

Luther caught himself for a second and allowed his anger to settle in. As if buying a calendar was the only measure of his pride in the local police force. As if forking over a bribe in the middle of his living room was proof that he, Luther Krank, stood solidly behind the boys in blue.

"I paid thirteen hundred bucks in city taxes last year," Luther said, his eyes flashing hot and settling on young Treen. "A portion of which went to pay your salary. Another portion went to pay the firemen, the ambulance drivers, the schoolteachers, the sanitation workers, the street cleaners, the Mayor and his rather comprehensive staff, the judges, the bailiffs, the jailers, all those clerks down at city hall, all those folks down at Mercy Hospital. They do a great job. You, sir, do a great job. I'm proud of all our city employees. But what's a calendar got to do with anything?"

Of course Treen had never had it put to him in such a logical manner, and he had no response. Salino either, for that matter. A tense pause followed.

Since Treen could think of no intelligent retort, he grew hot too and decided he would get Krank's license plate number and lie in ambush somewhere, maybe catch him speeding or sneaking through a stop sign. Pull him over, wait for a sarcastic comment, yank him out, sprawl him across the hood while cars eased by, slap the handcuffs on him, haul him to jail.

Such pleasant thoughts made Treen smile. Salino, however, was not smiling. He'd heard the rumors about Luther Krank and his goofy plans for Christmas. Frohmeyer'd told him. He'd driven by the night before and seen the handsome undecorated house with no Frosty, just sitting alone, peacefully yet oddly so different.

"I'm sorry you feel that way," Salino said, sadly. "We're just trying to raise a little extra to help needy kids."

Nora wanted to burst through the door and say, "Here's a check! Give me the calendar!" But she didn't, because the aftermath would not be pleasant.

Luther nodded with jaws clenched, eyes unflinching, and Treen began a rather dramatic rerolling of the calendar that would now be hawked to someone else. Under the weight of his large paws it popped and crinkled as it became smaller and smaller. Finally, it was as narrow as a broomstick and Treen slid it back into its tube and stuck a cap on the end. Ceremony over, it was time for them to leave.

"Merry Christmas," Salino said.

"Do the police still sponsor that softball team for orphans?" Luther asked.

"We certainly do," Treen replied.

"Then come back in the spring and I'll give you a hundred bucks for uniforms."

This did nothing to appease the officers. They couldn't bring themselves to say, "Thanks." Instead, they nodded and looked at each other.

Things were stiff as Luther got them out the door, nothing said, just the irritating sound of Treen tapping the tube against his leg, like a bored cop with a nightstick look-ing for a head to bash.

"It was only a hundred dollars," Nora said sharply as she reentered the room. Luther was peeking around the curtains, making sure they were indeed leaving.

"No, dear, it was much more," he said smugly, as if the situation had been complex and only he had the full grasp of it. "How about some yogurt?"

To the starving, the prospect of food erased all other thoughts. Each night they rewarded themselves with a small container of bland, fat-free, imitation fruit yogurt, which they savored like a last meal. Luther was down seven pounds and Nora six.

. . .

They were touring the neighborhood in a pickup truck, looking for targets. Ten of them were in the back, resting on bales of hay, singing as they rolled along. Under the quilts hands were being held and thighs groped, but harmless fun, at least for the moment. They were, after all, from the Lutheran church. Their leader was behind the wheel, and next to her was the minister's wife, who also played the organ on Sunday mornings.

The truck turned onto Hemlock, and the target quickly became obvious. They slowed as they neared the unadorned home of the Kranks. Luckily, Walt Scheel was outside wrestling with an extension cord that lacked about eight feet in connecting the electricity from his garage to his boxwoods, around which he had carefully woven four hundred new green lights. Since Krank wasn't decorating, he, Scheel, had decided to do so with extra gusto.

"Are those folks home?" the driver asked Walt as the truck came to a stop. She was nodding at the Kranks' place.

"Yes. Why?"

"Oh, we're out caroling. We got a youth group here from the Lutheran church, St. Mark's."

Walt suddenly smiled and dropped the extension cord. How lovely, he thought. Krank just thinks he can run from Christmas.

"Are they Jewish?" she asked.

"No."

"Buddhist or anything like that?"

"No, not at all. Methodist actually. They're trying to avoid Christmas this year."

"Do what?"

"You heard me." Walt was standing next to the driver's door, all smiles. "He's kind of a weird one. Skipping Christmas so he can save his money for a cruise."

The driver and the minister's wife looked long and hard at the Krank home across the street. The kids in the back had stopped singing and were listening to every word. Wheels were turning.

"I think some Christmas carolers would do them good," Scheel added helpfully. "Go on."

The truck emptied as the choir rushed onto the sidewalk. They stopped near the Kranks' mailbox. "Closer," Scheel yelled. "They won't mind."

They lined up near the house, next to Luther's favorite flower bed. Scheel ran to his front door and told Bev to call Frohmeyer.

Luther was scraping the sides of his yogurt container when a racket commenced very close to him. The carolers struck quick and loud with the opening stanza of "God Rest Ye Merry Gentlemen," and the Kranks ducked for cover. Then they darted from the kitchen, staying low, Luther in the lead with Nora on his back, into the living room and close to the front window, where, thankfully, the curtains were closed.

The choir waved excitedly when Luther was spotted peeking out.

"Christmas carolers," Luther hissed, taking a step back. "Right out there next to our junipers."

"How lovely," Nora said very quietly.

"Lovely? They're trespassing on our property. It's a setup."

"They're not trespassing."

"Of course they are. They're on our property without being invited. Someone told them to come, probably Frohmeyer or Scheel."

"Christmas carolers are not trespassers," Nora insisted, practically whispering.

"I know what I'm talking about."

"Then call your friends down at the police department."

"I might do that," Luther mused, peeking out again.

"Not too late to buy a calendar."

The entire Frohmeyer clan came running, Spike leading the pack on a skateboard, and by the time they fell in behind the carolers the Trogdons had heard the noise and were joining the commotion. Then the Beckers with the mother-in-law in tow and Rocky the dropout lagging behind her.

"Jingle Bells" was next, a lively and loud rendition, no doubt inspired by the excitement being created. The choir director motioned for the neighbors to join in, which they happily did, and by the time they began "Silent Night" their number had ballooned to at least thirty. The carolers hit most of their notes; the neighbors couldn't have cared less. They sang loudly so that old Luther in there would squirm.

After twenty minutes, Nora's nerves gave way, and she went to the shower. Luther pretended to read a magazine in his easy chair, but each carol was louder than the last. He fumed and cursed under his breath. The last time he peeked out there were people all over his front lawn, everyone smiling and shrieking at his house.

When they started with "Frosty the Snowman," he went to his office in the basement and found the cognac.

Eight

....

$\mathcal{L}$uther's morning routine hadn't changed in the eighteen years he'd lived on Hemlock. Up at six, slippers and bathrobe, brew the coffee, out the garage door, down the driveway where Milton the paperboy had left the *Gazette* an hour earlier. Luther could count the steps from the coffeepot to the newspaper, knowing they wouldn't vary by two or three. Back inside, a cup with just a trace of cream, the Sports section, then Metro, Business, and always last, the national and international news. Halfway through the obituaries, he would take a cup of coffee, the same lavender cup every day, with two sugars, to his dear wife.

On the morning after the caroling party on his front

lawn, Luther shuffled half-asleep down his drive and was about to pick up the *Gazette* when he saw a bright collection of colors out of the corner of his left eye. There was a sign in the center of his lawn. FREE FROSTY the damned thing proclaimed, in bold black letters. It was on white poster board, reds and greens around the borders, with a sketch of Frosty chained and shackled somewhere in a basement, no doubt the Kranks' basement. It was either a bad design by an adult with too much time to spare, or a rather good design by a kid with a mom looking over his shoulder.

Luther suddenly felt eyes watching him, lots of eyes, so he casually stuck the *Gazette* under his arm and strolled back into the house as if he'd seen nothing. He grumbled as he poured his coffee, cursed mildly as he took his chair. He couldn't enjoy Sports or Metro—even the obituaries couldn't hold his attention. Then he realized that Nora should not see the poster. She'd worry about it much more than he did.

With each new assault on his right to do as he pleased, Luther was more determined to ignore Christmas. He was concerned about Nora, though. He would never break, but he feared she would. If she believed the neighborhood children were now protesting, she just might collapse.

He struck quickly—slinking through the garage, cutting around the corner, high-stepping across the lawn because the grass was wet and practically frozen, yanking the poster from the ground, and tossing it into the utility room, where he'd deal with it later.

He took Nora her coffee, then settled once again at the kitchen table, where he tried in vain to concentrate on the *Gazette*. He was angry, though, and his feet were frozen.

Luther drove to work.

He had once advocated closing the office from the middle of December until after January 1. No one works anyway, he'd argued rather brilliantly at a firm meeting. The secretaries needed to shop so they left for lunch early, returned late, then left an hour later to run errands. Simply make everyone take their vacations in December, he had said forcefully. Sort of a two-week layoff, with pay of course. Billings were down anyway, he had explained with charts and graphs to back him up. Their clients certainly weren't in their offices, so no item of business could ever be finalized until the first week of January. Wiley & Beck could save a few bucks by avoiding the Christmas dinner and the office party. He had even passed out an article from *The Wall Street Journal* about a big firm in Seattle that had adopted such a policy, with outstanding results, or so said the *Journal*.

It had been a splendid presentation by Luther. The firm voted eleven to two against him, and he'd stewed for a month. Only Yank Slader'd hung in there with him.

Luther went through the motions of another morning, his mind on last night's concert by his junipers and the protest sign in his front yard. He enjoyed life on Hemlock, got on well with his neighbors, even managing to be cordial to Walt Scheel, and was uncomfortable now being the target of their displeasure.

Biff, the travel agent, changed his mood when she waltzed into his office with barely a knock—Dox, his secretary, was lost in catalogs—and presented their flight and cruise tickets, along with a handsome itinerary and an updated brochure on the *Island Princess*. She was gone in seconds, much too brief a stay to suit Luther, who, when he admired her figure and tan, couldn't help but dream of the countless string bikinis he would soon encounter. He locked his door and was soon lost in the warm blue waters of the Caribbean.

For the third time that week Luther sneaked away just before lunch and raced to the mall. He parked as far away as possible because he needed the hike, down eight pounds now and feeling very fit, and entered through Sears with a mob of other noontime shoppers. Except Luther was there for a nap.

Behind thick sunshades, he ducked into Tans Forever on the upper concourse. Daisy with the copper skin had been relieved by Daniella, a pale redhead whose constant tanning had only made her freckles expand and spread. She punched his card, assigned him to Salon 2, and, with all the wisdom of a highly skilled dermatologist, said, "I think twenty-two minutes should do it today, Luther." She was at least thirty years his junior, but had no problem addressing him simply as Luther. A kid working a temporary job for minimum wage, it never crossed her mind that perhaps she should call him Mr. Krank.

Why not twenty-one minutes? he wanted to snap. Or twenty-three?

He grumbled over his shoulder and went to Salon 2.

The FX-2000 BronzeMat was cool to the touch, a very good sign because Luther couldn't stand the thought of crawling into the thing after someone else had just left. He quickly sprayed it with Windex, wiped it furiously, then rechecked the locked door, undressed as if someone might see him, and very delicately crawled into the tanning bed.

He stretched and adjusted until things were as comfortable as they would get, then pulled the top down, hit the On switch, and began to bake. Nora'd been twice and wasn't sure she'd tan again because halfway through her last session someone rattled the doorknob and gave her a start. She blurted something, couldn't remember exactly what due to the terror of the moment, and as she instinctively jerked upward she cracked her head on the top of the BronzeMat.

Luther'd been blamed for that too. Laughing about it hadn't helped him.

Before long he was drifting away, drifting to the *Island Princess* with its four pools and dark, fit bodies lounging around, drifting to the white sandy beaches of Jamaica and Grand Cayman, drifting through the warm still waters of the Caribbean.

A buzzer startled him. His twenty-two minutes were up. Three sessions now and Luther could finally see some improvement in the rickety mirror on the wall. Just a matter of time before someone around the office commented on his tan. They were all so envious.

As he hurried back to work, his skin still warm, his

stomach even flatter after another skipped meal, it began to
sleet.

. . .

Luther caught himself dreading the drive home.
Things were fine until he turned onto Hemlock. Next door,
Becker was adding more lights to his shrubs, and, for spite,
he was emphasizing the end of his lawn next to Luther's
garage. Trogdon had so many lights you couldn't tell if he
was adding more, but Luther suspected he was. Across the
street, next door to Trogdon, Walt Scheel was decorating
more each day. This from a guy who'd hardly hung the first
strand a year ago.

And now, next door—on the east side of the Kranks'—
Swade Kerr had suddenly been seized with the spirit of
Christmas and was wrapping his scrawny little boxwoods
with brand-new red and green blinking lights. The Kerrs
homeschooled their brood of children and generally kept
them locked in the basement. They refused to vote, did
yoga, ate only vegetables, wore sandals with thick socks in
the wintertime, avoided employment, and claimed to be
atheists. Very crunchy, but not bad neighbors. Swade's wife,
Shirley, with a hyphenated last name, had trust funds.

"They've got me surrounded," Luther muttered to
himself as he parked in his garage, then sprinted into the
house and locked the door behind him.

"Look at these," Nora said with a frown, and after a
peck on the cheek, the obligatory "How was your day?"

Two pastel-colored envelopes, the obvious. "What is

it?" he snapped. The last thing Luther wanted to see was Christmas cards with their phony little messages. Luther wanted food, which tonight would be baked fish with steamed veggies.

He pulled out both cards, each with a Frosty on the front. Nothing was signed. No return address on the envelope.

Anonymous Christmas cards.

"Very funny," he said, flinging them onto the table.

"I thought you'd like them. They were postmarked in the city."

"It's Frohmeyer," Luther said, yanking off his tie. "He loves a practical joke."

Halfway through dinner, the doorbell rang. A couple of large bites and Luther could've cleaned his plate, but Nora was preaching the virtues of eating slowly. He was still hungry when he got to his feet and mumbled something about who could it be now?

The fireman's name was Kistler and the medic was Kendall, both young and lean, in great shape from countless hours pumping iron down at the station, no doubt at taxpayer expense, Luther thought to himself as he invited them inside, just barely through the front door. It was another annual ritual, another perfect example of what was wrong with Christmas.

Kistler's uniform was navy and Kendall's was olive. Neither matched the red-and-white Santa's hats both were wearing, but then who really cared? The hats were cute and whimsical, but Luther wasn't smiling. The medic held the paper bag down by his leg.

"Selling fruitcakes again this year, Mr. Krank," Kistler was saying. "Do it every year."

"Money goes for the toy drive," Kendall said with perfect timing.

"Our goal is nine thousand bucks."

"Last year we raised just over eight."

"Hitting it harder this year."

"Christmas Eve, we'll deliver toys to six hundred kids."

"It's an awesome project."

Back and forth, back and forth. A well-drilled tag team.

"You ought to see their faces."

"I wouldn't miss it for the world."

"Anyway, gotta raise the money, and fast."

"Got the old faithful, Mabel's Fruitcakes." Kendall sort of waved the bag at Luther as if he might want to grab it and take a peek inside.

"World-famous."

"They make 'em in Hermansburg, Indiana, home of Mabel's Bakery."

"Half the town works there. Make nothing but fruitcakes."

Those poor folks, Luther thought.

"They have a secret recipe, use only the freshest ingredients."

"And make the best fruitcake in the world."

Luther hated fruitcakes. The dates, figs, prunes, nuts, little bits of dried, colored fruit.

"Been making 'em for eighty years now."

"Best-selling cake in the country. Six tons last year."

Luther was standing perfectly still, holding his ground, his eyes darting back and forth, back and forth.

"No chemicals, no additives."

"I don't know how they keep them so fresh."

With chemicals and additives, Luther wanted to say.

A sharp bolt of hunger hit Luther hard. His knees almost buckled, his poker face almost grimaced. For two weeks now his sense of smell had been much keener, no doubt a side effect of a strict diet. Maybe he got a whiff of Mabel's finest, he wasn't sure, but a craving came over him. Suddenly, he had to have something to eat. Suddenly, he wanted to snatch the bag from Kendall, rip open a package, and start gnawing on a fruitcake.

And then it passed. With his jaws clenched, Luther hung on until it was gone, then he relaxed. Kistler and Kendall were so busy with their routine that they hadn't noticed.

"We get only so many."

"They're so popular they have to be rationed."

"We're lucky to get nine hundred."

"Ten bucks a pop, and we're at nine thousand for the toys."

"You bought five last year, Mr. Krank."

"Can you do it again?"

Yes, I bought five last year, Luther was now remembering. Took three to the office and secretly placed them on the desks of three colleagues. By the end of the week, they'd been passed around so much the packages were worn. Dox tossed them in the wastebasket when they shut down for Christmas.

Nora gave the other two to her hairdresser, a three-hundred-pound lady who collected them by the dozen and had fruitcake until July.

"No," Luther finally said. "I'll pass this year."

The tag team went silent. Kistler looked at Kendall and Kendall looked at Kistler.

"Say what?"

"I don't want any fruitcakes this year."

"Is five too many?" Kistler asked.

"One is too many," Luther replied, then slowly folded his arms across his chest.

"None?" Kendall asked, in disbelief.

"Zero," Luther said.

They looked as pitiful as possible.

"You guys still put on that Fourth of July fishing rodeo for handicapped kids?" Luther asked.

"Every year," said Kistler.

"Great. Come back in the summer and I'll donate a hundred bucks for the fishing rodeo."

Kistler managed to mumble a very weak "Thanks."

It took a few awkward movements to get them out the door. Luther returned to the kitchen table, where everything was gone—Nora, his plate with the last two bites of steamed fish, his glass of water, his napkin. Everything. Furious, he stormed the pantry, where he found a jar of peanut butter and some stale saltines.

Nine

....

○

$\mathcal{S}$tanley Wiley's father had
founded Wiley & Beck in 1949. Beck had been dead so
long now no one knew exactly why his name was still on the
door. Had a nice ring to it—Wiley & Beck—and, too, it
would be expensive to change the stationery and such. For
an accounting firm that had been around for half a century,
the amazing thing was how little it had grown. There were
a dozen partners in tax, including Luther, and twenty or so
in auditing. Their clients were mid-range companies that
couldn't afford the national accounting firms.

If Stanley Wiley'd had more ambition, some thirty
years earlier, the old firm might possibly have caught the
wave and become a force. But he hadn't, and it didn't, and

now it pretended to be content by calling itself a "boutique firm."

Just as Luther was planning another quick departure for another sprint to the mall, Stanley materialized from nowhere with a long sandwich, lettuce hanging off the sides. "Got a minute?" he said with a mouthful. He was already sitting before Luther could say yes or no or can it be quick? He wore silly bow ties and usually had a variety of stains on his blue button-downs—ink, mayonnaise, coffee. Stanley was a slob, his office a notorious landfill where documents and files were lost for months. "Try Stanley's office" was the firm's slogan for paperwork that would never be found.

"I hear you're not going to be at the Christmas dinner tomorrow night," he said, still chewing. Stanley liked to roam the halls at lunch with a sandwich in one hand, a soda in the other, as if he were too busy for a real lunch.

"I'm eliminating a lot of things this year, Stanley, no offense to anyone," Luther said.

"So it's true."

"It's true. We will not be there."

Stanley swallowed with a frown, then examined the sandwich in search of the next bite. He was the managing partner, not the boss. Luther'd been a partner for six years. No one at Wiley & Beck could force him to do anything.

"Sorry to hear that. Jayne will be disappointed."

"I'll drop her a note," Luther said. It wasn't a terrible evening—a nice dinner at an old restaurant downtown, in a private room upstairs, good food, decent wines, a few speeches, then a band and dancing until late. Black tie, of course, and the ladies tried hard to one-up each other with dresses and jewelry. Jayne Wiley was a delightful woman who deserved a lot more than she got with Stanley.

"Any particular reason?" Stanley asked, prying just a little.

"We're skipping the whole production this year, Stanley, no tree, no gifts, no hassle. Saving the money and taking a cruise for ten days. Blair's gone, we need a break. I figure we'll catch up rather nicely next year, or if not, the year after."

"It does come every year, doesn't it?"

"It does indeed."

"I see you're losing weight."

"Ten pounds. The beaches are waiting."

"You look great, Luther. Tanning, I hear."

"Trying a darker shade, yes. I can't let the sun get the best of me."

A huge bite of the ham-on-baguette, with strands of lettuce trailing along and hanging between the lips. Then movement: "Not a bad idea, really." Or something like that.

Stanley's idea of a vacation was a week in his beach house, a hand-me-down in which he had invested nothing in thirty years. Luther and Nora had spent one dreadful week there, guests of the Wileys, who took the main bedroom and put the Kranks in the "guest suite," a narrow room with bunk beds and no air conditioning. Stanley'd knocked back gin and tonics from midmorning until late afternoon and the sun never touched his skin.

He left, his cheeks full, but before Luther could escape, Yank Slader darted in. "Up to fifty-two hundred bucks, old boy," he announced. "With no end in sight. Abigail just spent six hundred bucks on a dress for the Christmas dinner, don't know why she couldn't wear the one from last year or the year before, but why argue? Shoes were a buck-forty. Purse another ninety. Closets're full of purses and shoes, but don't get me started. We'll top seven grand at this rate. Please let me go on the cruise."

Inspired by Luther, Yank was keeping a precise tally on the Christmas damage. Twice a week he dashed in for updates. What he would do with the results was uncertain. Most likely nothing, and he knew it. "You're my hero," he said again, and left as quickly as he'd arrived.

They're all envious, Luther thought to himself. At this moment, crunch time with only a week to go, and the holiday madness growing each day, they're all jealous as hell. Some, like Stanley, were reluctant to admit it. Others, like Yank, were downright proud of Luther.

Too late to tan. Luther walked to his window and enjoyed the view of a cold rain falling on the city. Gray skies, barren trees, a few leaves scattering with the wind, traffic backed up on the streets in the distance. How lovely, he thought smugly. He patted his flat stomach, then went downstairs and had a diet soda with Biff, the travel agent.

• • •

At the buzzer, Nora bolted from the BronzeMat and grabbed a towel. Sweating was not something she particularly enjoyed, and she wiped herself with a vengeance.

She was wearing a very small red bikini, one that had looked great on the young slinky model in the catalog, one she knew she'd never wear in public but Luther had insisted on anyway. He'd gawked at the model and threatened to order the thing himself. It wasn't too expensive, so Nora now owned it.

She glanced in the mirror and again blushed at the sight of herself in such a skimpy garment. Sure she was losing weight. Sure she was getting a tan. But it would take five years of starvation and hard labor in the gym to do justice to what she was wearing at that moment.

She dressed quickly, pulling her slacks and sweater on over the bikini. Luther swore he tanned in the nude, but she wasn't stripping for anyone.

Even dressed, she still felt like a slut. The thing was tight in all the wrong places, and when she walked, well, it wasn't exactly comfortable. She couldn't wait to race home, take it off, throw it away, and enjoy a long hot bath.

She'd made it safely out of Tans Forever and rounded a corner when she came face to face with the Reverend Doug Zabriskie, their minister. He was laden with shopping bags, while she held nothing but her overcoat. He was pale, she was red-faced and still sweating. He was comfortable in his old tweed jacket, overcoat, collar, black shirt. Nora's bikini was cutting off her circulation and shrinking by the moment.

They hugged politely. "Missed you last Sunday," he said, the same irritating habit he'd picked up years ago.

"We're so busy," she said, checking her forehead for sweat.

"Are you okay, Nora?"

"Fine," she snapped.

"You look a little winded."

"A lot of walking," she said, lying to her minister.

For some reason he glanced down at her shoes. She certainly wasn't wearing sneakers.

"Could we chat for a moment?" he asked.

"Well, sure," she said. There was an empty bench near the railing of the concourse. The Reverend lugged his bags over and piled them beside it. When Nora sat, Luther's little red bikini shifted again and something gave way, a strap perhaps, just above her hip, and something was sliding down there. Her slacks were loose, not tight at all, and there was plenty of room for movement.

"I've heard lots of rumors," he began softly. He had the annoying habit of getting close to your face when he spoke. Nora crossed and recrossed her legs, and with each maneuver made things worse.

"What kind of rumors?" she asked stiffly.

"Well, I'll be very honest, Nora," he said, leaning even lower and closer. "I hear it from a good source that you and Luther have decided not to observe Christmas this year."

"Sort of, yes."

"I've never heard of this," he said gravely, as if the Kranks had discovered a new variety of sin.

She was suddenly afraid to move, and even then got the impression that she was still falling out of her clothes. Fresh beads of sweat popped up along her forehead. "Are you okay, Nora?" he asked.

"I'm fine and we're fine. We still believe in Christmas,

in celebrating the birth of Christ, we're just passing on all the foolishness this year. Blair's gone and we're taking a break."

He pondered this long and hard, while she shifted slightly. "It is a bit crazy, isn't it?" he said, looking at the pile of shopping bags he had deposited nearby.

"Yes it is. Look, we're fine, Doug, I promise. We're happy and healthy and just relaxing a bit. That's all."

"I hear you're leaving."

"Yes, for ten days on a cruise."

He stroked his beard as though he wasn't sure if he approved of this or not.

"You won't miss the midnight service, will you?" he asked with a smile.

"No promises, Doug."

He patted her knee and said good-bye. She waited until he was out of sight, and then finally mustered the courage to get to her feet. She shuffled out of the mall, cursing Luther and his bikini.

. . .

Vic Frohmeyer's wife's cousin's youngest daughter was active in her Catholic church, which had a large youth choir that enjoyed caroling around the city. Couple of phone calls, and the gig was booked.

A light snow was falling when the concert began. The choir formed a half-moon in the driveway, near the gas lamp, and on cue started bawling "O Little Town of Bethlehem." They waved at Luther when he peeked through the blinds.

A crowd soon gathered behind the carolers, kids from the neighborhood, the Beckers from next door, the Trogdon clan. There by virtue of an anonymous tip, a reporter for the *Gazette* watched for a few minutes, then asserted himself and rang the Kranks' doorbell.

Luther yanked the door open, ready to land a punch. "What is it?" "White Christmas" resounded in the background.

"Are you Mr. Krank?" asked the reporter.

"Yes, and who are you?"

"Brian Brown with the *Gazette*. Can I ask you some questions?"

"About what?"

"About this skipping Christmas business."

Luther gazed at the crowd in his driveway. One of those dark silhouettes out there had squealed on him. One of his neighbors had called the newspaper. Either Frohmeyer or Walt Scheel.

"I'm not talking," he said and slammed the door. Nora was in the shower, again, and Luther went to the basement.

Ten

....

$\mathcal{L}$uther suggested dinner at Angelo's, their favorite Italian place. It was on the ground floor of an old building downtown, far away from the hordes at the malls and shopping centers, five blocks from the parade route. It was a good night to be away from Hemlock.

They ordered salad with light dressing and pasta with tomato sauce, no meat, no wine, no bread. Nora had tanned for the seventh time, Luther for the tenth, and as they sipped their sparkling water they admired their weathered looks and chuckled at all the pale faces around them. One of Luther's grandmothers had been half-Italian, and his Mediterranean genes were proving quite conducive to tanning. He was several shades darker than Nora, and his friends were noticing. He couldn't have cared less. By now, everybody knew they were headed for the islands.

"It's starting now," Nora said, looking at her watch.

Luther looked at his. Seven P.M.

The Christmas parade was launched every year from Veteran's Park, in midtown. With floats and fire trucks and marching bands, it never changed. Santa always brought up the rear in a sleigh built by the Rotarians and escorted by eight fat Shriners on mini-bikes. The parade looped through the west side and came close to Hemlock. Every year for the past eighteen, the Kranks and their neighbors had camped along the parade route and made an event out of it. It was a festive evening, one Luther and Nora wished to avoid this year.

Hemlock would be wild with kids and carolers and who knew what else. Probably bicycle gangs chanting "Free Frosty" and little terrorists planting signs on their front lawn.

"How was the firm's Christmas dinner?" Nora asked.

"Sounded like the usual. Same room, same waiters, same tenderloin, same soufflé. Slader said Stanley got drunk as a skunk during cocktails."

"I've never seen him sober during cocktails."

"He made the same speech—great effort, billings up, we'll knock 'em dead next year, Wiley & Beck is family, thanks to all. That sort of stuff. I'm glad we missed it."

"Anybody else skip it?"

"Slader said Maupin from auditing was a no-show."

"I wonder what Jayne wore?"

"I'll ask Slader. I'm sure he took notes."

Their salads arrived and they gawked at the baby spinach like famine refugees. But they slowly and properly applied the dressing, a little salt and pepper, then began eating as if they were completely disinterested in food.

The *Island Princess* served nonstop food. Luther planned to eat until he popped.

At a table not far away, a pretty young lady with dark hair was eating with her date. Nora saw her and laid down her fork.

"Do you think she's okay, Luther?" Luther glanced around the room and said, "Who?"

"Blair."

He finished chewing and pondered the question that she now asked only three times a day. "She's fine, Nora. She's having a great time."

"Is she safe?" Another standard question, posed as if Luther should know for certain whether their daughter was safe or not at that precise moment.

"The Peace Corps hasn't lost a volunteer in thirty years. Yes, trust me, they're very careful, Nora. Now eat."

She pushed her greens around, took a bite, lost interest. Luther wiped his plate clean and honed in on hers. "You gonna eat that?" he asked.

She swapped plates, and in a flash Luther had cleaned the second one. The pasta arrived and she guarded her bowl. After a few measured bites, she stopped suddenly, her fork halfway to her face. Then she laid it down again and said, "I forgot."

Luther was chewing with a vengeance. "What is it?" Her face was stricken with terror.

"What is it, Nora?" he repeated, swallowing hard.

"Don't those judges come around after the parade?"

Then it hit Luther too. He retired his fork for a moment, sipped water, gazed painfully at nothing in the distance. Yes, indeed, it was true.

After the parade, a committee from Parks and Rec toured the neighborhoods on a float pulled by a John Deere tractor and examined the level of Christmas spirit. They gave individual awards in various categories—Original Design, Festive Lighting, etc. And they handed out an award to the street with the best decorations. Hemlock had won the blue ribbon twice.

The year before, Hemlock had placed second, primarily because, according to the gossip on the street, two of the forty-two homes had not put up a Frosty. Boxwood Lane three blocks north had come from nowhere with a dazzling row of candy canes—Candy Cane Lane it described itself—and took away Hemlock's award. Frohmeyer circulated memos for a month.

Dinner, now ruined, came to a standstill as they picked through their pasta and killed as much time as possible. Two long cups of decaf. When Angelo's was empty, Luther paid the bill and they drove home, slowly.

. . .

Sure enough, Hemlock lost again. Luther fetched the *Gazette* in the semidarkness, and was horrified with the front page of Metro. The award winners were listed—

Cherry Avenue first, Boxwood Lane second, Stanton third. Trogdon across the street with more than fourteen thousand lights finished fourth in Festive Lighting.

In the center of the page was a large color photo of the Krank home, taken at some distance. Luther studied it intently and tried to determine the angle. The photographer had shot down and at a wide angle, sort of an aerial view.

Next door, the Becker house positively glowed with a blinding display of lights. On the other side, the Kerrs' house and lawn were perfectly lined with alternating reds and greens, thousands of them by now.

The Krank home was dark.

To the east, the Frohmeyers', Nugents', and Galdys' could be seen, all glowing warmly, all with their Frostys sitting snugly on the roofs. To the west, the Dents', Sloanes', and Bellingtons' all radiated Christmas splendor.

The Krank home was very dark.

"Scheel," Luther grumbled to himself. The photo was taken from directly across the street. Walt Scheel had allowed the photographer to climb onto the roof of his two-story house and shoot down with a wide lens. Probably had the whole street egging him on.

Under the photo was a brief story. Headlined "SKIPPING CHRISTMAS," it read:

The home of Mr. and Mrs. Luther Krank is rather dark this Christmas. While the rest of their neighbors on Hemlock Street are decorating and busily preparing for Santa, the Kranks are skipping Christmas and preparing for a cruise, according to unnamed sources. No tree, no lights, and no Frosty up on the roof, the only house on Hemlock to keep Frosty hidden in the basement. (Hemlock, a frequent winner in the *Gazette*'s street decoration contest, finished a disappointing sixth this year.) "I hope they're satisfied now," complained one unidentified neighbor. "A rotten display of selfishness," said another.

If Luther'd had a machine gun, he would've bolted outside and commenced spraying houses.

Instead he sat for a long time with a knot in his stomach and tried to convince himself that this too would pass. Just four days until they left, and when they came back all those damned Frostys would be stored away, the lights and trees would be gone. The bills would start flooding in, and perhaps then all his wonderful neighbors would be more sympathetic.

He flipped through the newspaper but his concentration was shot. Finally, Luther found his resolve, gritted his teeth, and took the bad news to his wife.

"What a horrible way to wake up," Nora said as she tried to focus on the photo in the newspaper. She rubbed her eyes and squinted.

"That jerk Scheel allowed the photographer to get on his roof," Luther said.

"Are you sure?"

"Of course I'm sure. Look at the picture."

She was trying. Then she found her focus and read the story. She gasped at ". . . rotten display of selfishness."

"Who said that?" she demanded.

"Either Scheel or Frohmeyer. Who knows. I'm in the shower."

"How dare they!" Nora said, still gawking at the photo.

Atta girl, thought Luther. Get mad. Stiffen your back. Just four days to go—we're not collapsing now.

. . .

That night, after dinner and an effort at television, Luther decided to take a walk. He bundled up and wrapped a wool scarf around his neck; it was below freezing outside with a chance of snow. He and Nora had bought one of the first homes on Hemlock; damned if he'd be forced to hide inside. This was his street, his neighborhood, his friends. One day soon this little episode would be forgotten.

Luther ambled along, hands stuck deep in his pockets, cold air invigorating his lungs.

He made it to the far end, to the intersection of Moss Point, before Spike Frohmeyer picked up his trail and caught him on a skateboard. "Hi, Mr. Krank," he said as he rolled to a stop.

"Well hello, Spike."

"What brings you out?"

"Just taking a little walk."

"Enjoying the Christmas decorations?"

"Of course. What brings you out?"

"Just watching the street," Spike said, then looked around as if an invasion were imminent.

"What's Santa gonna bring you?"

Spike smiled and pondered for a second. "Not sure, but probably a Gameboy and a hockey stick and a set of drums."

"Quite a haul."

"Course I don't really believe anymore, you know. But Mike's just five so we still pretend."

"Sure."

"Gotta go. Merry Christmas."

"Merry Christmas to you, Spike," Luther said, uttering the forbidden greeting for what he hoped was the first and last time of the season. Spike disappeared down Hemlock, no doubt racing home to report to his father that Mr. Krank was out of his house and loose on the sidewalk.

Luther stopped in front of the Trogdons' spectacle— more than fourteen thousand lights draped over trees and shrubs and windows and porch columns. Up on the roof with Frosty was Santa and his reindeer—Rudolph of course with a bright, flashing nose—all perfectly outlined with white lights. The roof itself was lined with two rows of red and green, blinking alternatively. The chimney was flashing too—hundreds of blue lights pulsating at once and casting an eerie glow over old Frosty. Along the holly bushes next to the house a squad of tin soldiers stood guard, each as tall as a human and wrapped with multicolored lights. In the center of the lawn was a handsome Nativity scene, complete with real hay bales and a goat whose tail went up and down.

Quite a show.

Luther heard something, a ladder falling in the garage next to the Trogdons'. The garage door was up and through the shadows he saw Walt Scheel wrestling with yet another strand of lights. He walked over and caught Walt off guard. "Evening, Walt," he said pleasantly.

"Well, if it isn't ole Scrooge himself," Walt said with a forced smile. They shook hands and each tried to think of something cutting and witty. Luther took a step back, looked up, and said, "How'd that photographer get up there?"

"Which photographer?"

"The one from the *Gazette.*"

"Oh, that one."

"Yes, that one."

"He climbed up."

"No kidding. Why'd you let him?"

"I don't know. Said he wanted to get the whole street."

Luther snorted and waved it off. "I'm a little surprised at you, Walt," he said, though he wasn't surprised at all. For eleven years they'd been cordial on the surface, neither wanting an outright feud. But Luther didn't like Walt for his snobbery and one-upmanship. And Walt didn't care for Luther because he'd suspected for years that their salaries were almost equal.

"And I'm a little surprised at you," Walt said, but neither neighbor was surprised at all.

"I think you have a light out over there," Luther said, pointing to a shrub wrapped with a hundred lights.

"I'll get right on it."

"See you," Luther said, walking away.

"Merry Christmas," Walt called after him.

"Yeah, yeah."

Eleven

....

$\mathcal{T}$he Wiley & Beck office Christmas party would begin with a lunch catered by two feuding Greek brothers who made the best baklava in the city. The bar opened at precisely eleven forty-five—three bars actually—and soon thereafter things got sloppy. Stanley Wiley would be the first to get smashed—he'd blame it on the loaded eggnog—and he'd stand on a box at the end of the conference table and deliver the same speech he'd given a week earlier at the black-tie Christmas dinner. Then they'd present him with a gift, a shotgun or a new sand wedge or some other useless souvenir that he'd practically cry over, then quietly give to a client months later. There'd be other gifts, some speeches and gags, and a song or two as the booze flowed. Two male strippers appeared one year, and, to the beat of a howling boom box, disrobed down to their leopard thongs while the men ran for cover and the secretaries squealed with delight. Dox, Luther's secretary, had squealed the loudest and still had photos of the boys. In a memo, Stanley had banned future strippers.

By five, some of the most starched and staid accountants at Wiley & Beck would be groping or attempting to grope some of the homeliest secretaries. Getting plastered was accepted behavior. They'd haul Stanley to his office and fill him with coffee before he could go home. The firm hired cars so no one would drive.

All in all, it was a mess. But the partners loved it because it was a good drunk away from their wives, who'd been properly entertained at the firm's fancy Christmas dinner and had never been invited to the office party. The secretaries loved it because they saw and heard things they could tuck away and use as blackmail for the rest of the year.

Luther hated the Christmas party even in a good year. He drank little and never got drunk, and every year he was embarrassed for his colleagues as they made fools of themselves.

So he stayed in his office with his door locked and tended to last-minute details. Then some music started down the hall just after 11 A.M. Luther found the right moment and disappeared. It was the twenty-third of December. He wouldn't return until the sixth of January, and by then the office would be back to normal.

Good riddance.

He stepped into the travel agency to say good-bye to Biff, but she was already gone, off to a fabulous new resort in Mexico that offered a holiday package. He walked briskly to his car, quite proud that he was skipping the madness up on the sixth floor. He drove toward the mall, for one last tanning session, one last look at the crush of idiots who'd waited till almost the last minute to buy whatever was left in the stores. The traffic was dense and slow, and when he finally arrived at the mall a traffic cop was blocking the entrance. Parking lots were full. No more room. Go away.

Gladly, thought Luther.

He met Nora for lunch at a crowded bakery in the District. They'd actually made a reservation, something unheard of for the rest of the year. He was late. She'd been crying.

"It's Bev Scheel," she said. "Went for a checkup yesterday. The cancer's back, for the third time."

Though Luther and Walt had never been close, their wives had managed to maintain good relations over the past couple of years. Truth was, for many years no one on Hemlock had much to do with the Scheels. They'd worked hard to have more, and their higher income had always been on display.

"It's spread to her lungs," Nora said, wiping her eyes. They ordered sparkling water. "And they suspect it's in her kidneys and liver."

Luther winced as the horrific disease crept on. "That's awful," he said in a low voice.

"This could be her last Christmas."

"Did her doctor say that?" he asked, wary of amateur prognostications.

"No, I did."

They dwelt on the Scheels far too long, and when Luther'd had enough he said, "We leave in forty-eight hours. Cheers." They touched plastic glasses and Nora managed a smile.

Halfway through their salads, Luther asked, "Any regrets?"

She shook her head no, swallowed, and said, "Oh, I've missed the tree at times, the decorations, the music, the memories, I guess. But not the traffic and shopping and stress. It was a great idea, Luther."

"I'm a genius."

"Let's not get carried away. You think Blair will even think about Christmas?"

"Not if she's lucky. Doubt it," he said with a mouthful. "She's working with a bunch of heathen savages who worship rivers and such. Why should they take a break for Christmas?"

"That's a little harsh, Luther. Savages?"

"Just kidding, dear. I'm sure they're gentle people. Not to worry."

"She said she never looks at a calendar."

"Now that's impressive. I've got two calendars in my office and I still forget which day it is."

Millie from the Women's Clinic barged in with a hug for Nora and a Merry Christmas for Luther, who would've otherwise been irritated except that Millie was tall and lanky and very cute for a woman her age. Early fifties.

"You heard about Bev Scheel," Millie whispered as if Luther had suddenly vanished. Now he was irritated. He prayed he'd never be stricken with some dreadful disease, not in this city. The volunteer women would know about it before he did.

Give me a heart attack or a car wreck, something quick. Something that cannot be whispered about while I linger.

Millie finally left, and they finished their salads. Luther was famished as he paid the check, and caught himself once again dreaming of the luxurious spreads of food in the *Island Princess* brochures.

Nora had errands to run. Luther did not. He drove to Hemlock, parked in his driveway, a little relieved that there were no neighbors loitering near his house. In the daily mail there were four more anonymous Frosty Christmas cards, these postmarked in Rochester, Fort Worth, Green Bay, and St. Louis. Frohmeyer's bunch at the university traveled a lot, and Luther suspected this was their little game. Frohmeyer was restless and creative enough to mastermind such a prank. Thirty-one Frosty cards had now been received, two all the way from Vancouver. Luther was saving them, and when he returned from the Caribbean he planned to stuff them in a large envelope and mail them, anonymously of course, to Vic Frohmeyer, two doors down.

"They'll arrive with all of his credit card bills," Luther said to himself as he put the Frosty cards in a drawer with the others. He made a fire, settled under a quilt in his chair, and fell asleep.

It was a rowdy night on Hemlock. Marauding bands of boisterous carolers took turns at the Krank house. Often they were assisted by neighbors seized by the spirit of the moment. At one point, a chant of "We Want Frosty!" erupted behind a choir from the Lions Club.

Handmade signs demanding "Free Frosty" appeared, the first hammered into the ground by none other than Spike Frohmeyer. He and his little gang were up and down Hemlock, on skateboards and bikes, yelling and reveling in their pre–Christmas Eve exuberance.

An impromptu block party materialized. Trish Trogdon fixed hot cocoa for the kids while her husband, Wes, rigged up speakers in the driveway. Soon "Frosty the Snowman" and "Jingle Bells" were wafting through the night, interrupted only when a real choir arrived to serenade the Kranks. Wes played a selection of favorites, but his favorite that night was "Frosty."

The Krank home remained dark and quiet, locked and secure. Nora was in the bedroom gathering what she wanted to pack. Luther was in the basement, trying to read.

Twelve

....

$\mathcal{C}$hristmas Eve. Luther and
Nora slept until almost 7 A.M., when the phone awakened
them. "May I speak to Frosty?" came the voice of a
teenager, and before Luther could shoot back a retort the
line was dead. He managed to laugh though, and as he
jumped out of bed he patted his rather firm stomach and
said, "The islands are calling us, dear. Let's pack."

"Fetch my coffee," she said and slid deeper under the
covers.

The morning was overcast and cold, the chance of a
white Christmas fifty-fifty. Luther certainly didn't want
one. Nora would lapse into a spell of nostalgia if snow fell

on Christmas Eve. She'd grown up in Connecticut, where, according to her, every Christmas had been white.

Luther didn't want the weather meddling with their flight tomorrow.

He stood at the front window, exactly where the tree would've been, sipped his coffee, gazed upon his lawn to make sure it had not been vandalized by Spike Frohmeyer and his band of outlaws, and looked at the Scheel home across the street. In spite of all its lights and decorations, it was a gloomy place. Walt and Bev were in there, having their coffee, sleepwalking through the motions, both knowing but not saying that this could be their last Christmas together. For a moment Luther felt a twinge of regret about eliminating Christmas, but it didn't last long.

Next door, things were certainly different at the Trogdons'. They followed the odd custom of playing Santa Claus on the morning of Christmas Eve, twenty-four hours before the rest of the world, then loading their mini-van and racing off to a lodge for a week of skiing. Same lodge every year, and Trogdon had explained that they had Christmas dinner in a stone cabin before a roaring fireplace with thirty other Trogdons. Very cozy, great skiing, kids loved it, and the family got along.

Different strokes.

So the Trogdons were already up and unwrapping piles of gifts. Luther could see movement around their tree, and he knew that before long they'd be hauling boxes and bags to the van, then the yelling would start. The Trodgon kids would be whisked away before they were forced to explain, how, exactly, they got such a favorable deal from Santa Claus.

Otherwise, Hemlock was still and quiet, bracing itself for the festivities.

Luther took another sip and grinned smugly at the world. On the morning of a typical Christmas Eve, Nora would bounce out of bed at sunrise with two long lists, one for her, an even longer one for him. By seven, she'd have a turkey in the oven, the house spotless, the tables set for the party, and her thoroughly defeated husband out in the jungle trying to beat last-minute traffic with his list. They'd bark at each other, face to face and by cell phone. He'd forget something and be sent back into the streets. He'd break something and the world would come to an end.

Total chaos. Then, around six, when they were both exhausted and sick of the holidays, their guests would arrive. Their guests would also be dog-tired from the frenzied ordeal of Christmas, but they would push on and make the best of it.

The Krank Christmas party had begun years earlier with a dozen or so friends over for appetizers and drinks. Last year, they'd fed fifty.

His smug smile spread even wider across his face. He relished the solitude of his home and the prospect of a day with nothing to do but throw a few clothes in a suitcase and get ready for the beaches.

They enjoyed a late breakfast of tasteless bran cereal and yogurt. Conversation over the *Gazette* was soft and pleasant. Nora was trying gamely to ignore the memories of past Christmases. She worked hard at being excited about their trip.

"Do you think she's safe?" she finally asked.

"She's fine," Luther said without looking up.

They stood at the front window and talked about the Scheels, and they watched the Trogdons move about. Traffic picked up on Hemlock as folks ventured out for one last foray into the madness. A delivery truck stopped in front of their house. Butch the deliveryman bounded out of it with a box. He ran to the front door just as Luther was opening it.

"Merry Christmas," he said tersely, and practically threw the package at Luther. A week earlier, during a less-stressful delivery, Butch had lingered a bit, waiting for his annual gratuity. Luther had explained that they were not celebrating Christmas this year. See, we have no tree, Butch. No decorations. No gifts. No lights on the shrubs, no Frosty on the roof. Just dropping out this year, Butch. No calendars from the police, no fruitcakes from the firemen. Nothing, Butch.

Butch left with nothing.

The box was from a mail-order outfit called Boca Beach. Luther'd found them on the Internet. He took the package to the bedroom, locked the door, and put on a matching shirt and shorts outfit that in print had looked just a little offbeat, but now, hanging on Luther, looked downright gaudy.

"What is it, Luther?" Nora said, banging on the door.

It was a yellow, aqua, and teal print of marine life—large fat fishes with bubbles floating up from their mouths. Whimsical, yes. Silly, yes.

And Luther decided right there on the spot that he would love it and wear it proudly around one of the pools on the *Island Princess.* He yanked open the door. Nora covered her mouth and was instantly hysterical. He paraded down the hall, wife behind him in stitches, his brown feet and toes a sharp contrast to the khaki carpet, and he marched into the living room where he stood proudly at the front window for all of Hemlock to see.

"You're not going to wear that!" Nora roared from behind him.

"I certainly am!"

"Then I'm not going!"

"Yes you are."

"It's hideous."

"You're just jealous because you don't have this outfit."

"I'm thrilled that I don't have it."

He grabbed her and they danced around the room, both laughing, Nora to the point of having tears in her eyes. Her husband, an uptight tax accountant with a stodgy outfit like Wiley & Beck, trying his best to dress like a beach bum. And missing badly.

The phone rang.

As Luther would remember after, he and Nora stopped their dancing and laughing on the second ring, maybe the third, and for some reason paused and stared at the phone. It rang again, and he walked a few steps to get it. Things were deathly still and quiet; as he recalled later, everything seemed to be in slow motion.

"Hello," he said. For some reason, the receiver felt heavier.

"Daddy, it's me."

He was surprised, then he was not. Surprised to hear Blair's voice, but then not surprised at all that she had schemed some way to get to a phone to call her parents and wish them a Merry Christmas. They had phones in Peru, after all.

But her words were so crisp and clear. Luther had trouble picturing his beloved daughter on a stump in the jungle yelling into some portable satellite phone.

"Blair," he said. Nora bolted to his side.

The next word that registered with Luther was the word "Miami." There were words before it and some after, but that one stuck. Just seconds into the conversation Luther was treading water and about to sink. Things were swirling.

"How are you, dear?" he asked.

A few words, then that "Miami" word again.

"You're in Miami?" Luther said, his voice high and dry. Nora shuffled quickly so that her eyes, wild and harsh, were just inches from his.

Then he listened. Then he repeated, "You're in Miami, coming home for Christmas. How wonderful, Blair!" Nora's jaws unlocked, her mouth fell open as wide as Luther had ever seen it.

More listening, then "Who? Enrique?" Then at full volume, Luther said, "Your fiancé! But what fiancé?!"

Nora somehow managed to think, and she pushed the

Speaker button on the phone. Blair's words poured forward and echoed around the living room: "He's a Peruvian doctor I met right after I got here, and he's just so wonderful. We fell in love at first sight and within a week decided to get married. He's never been to the States and he's so excited. I've told him all about Christmas there—the tree, the decorations, Frosty up on the roof, the Christmas party, everything. Is it snowing, Daddy? Enrique has never seen a white Christmas."

"No, honey, not yet. Here's your mother." Luther handed the receiver to Nora, who took it, though with the Speaker button down it wasn't needed.

"Blair, where are you, dear?" Nora asked, doing a good job of sounding enthused.

"In the Miami airport, Mom, and our flight gets home at six-oh-three. Mom, you're gonna love Enrique, he's the sweetest thing, and drop-dead gorgeous, too. We're crazy in love with each other. We'll talk about the wedding, probably do it next summer, don't you think?"

"Uh, we'll see."

Luther had fallen onto the sofa, apparently stricken with a life-threatening ailment.

Blair gushed on: "I've told him all about Christmas on Hemlock, the kids, the Frostys, the big party at our house. You're doing the party, aren't you, Mom?"

Luther, near death, groaned, and Nora made her first mistake. In the panic of the moment she could not be blamed for muddled thinking. What she should've said, what she wished she'd said, what Luther later, with perfect hindsight, claimed she should've said, was "Well, no, honey, we're not doing the party this year."

But nothing was clear right then, and Nora said, "Of course we are."

Luther groaned again. Nora looked at him, the fallen beach bum in his ridiculous costume, lying over there like he'd been shot. She'd certainly shoot him if given half a chance.

"Oh great! Enrique has always wanted to see Christmas in the States. I've told him all about it. Isn't this a wonderful surprise, Mom?"

"Oh, honey, I'm so thrilled," Nora managed to get out with just enough conviction. "We'll have a grand time."

"Mom, no gifts, okay. Please promise me no gifts. I wanted to surprise you by coming home, but I don't want you and Daddy running around right now buying a bunch of gifts. Promise?"

"I promise."

"Great. I can't wait to get home."

You've been gone only a month, Luther wanted to say.

"Are you sure this is okay, Mom?" As if Luther and Nora had a choice. As if they could say, "No, Blair, you can't come home for Christmas. Turn around, dear, and go back to the jungles of Peru."

"I gotta run. We fly from here to Atlanta, then home. Can you meet us?"

"Of course, dear," Nora said. "No problem. And you say he's a doctor?"

"Yes, Mother, and he's so wonderful."

Luther sat on the edge of the sofa with his face stuck in his palms and appeared to be crying. Nora stood with the phone clutched in her hand and her hands on her hips, staring at the man on the sofa and debating whether or not to hurl it at him.

Against her better judgment, she decided not to.

He opened his palms just wide enough to say, "What time is it?"

"It's eleven-fifteen, December twenty-fourth."

The room was frozen for a long time before Luther said, "Why did you tell her we were having the party?"

"Because we're having the party."

"Oh."

"I don't know who's coming or what they're going to eat when they get here, but we're having a party."

"I'm not sure—"

"Don't start, Luther. This was your stupid idea."

"You didn't think it was stupid yesterday."

"Yeah, well today you're an idiot. We're having the party, Mr. Beach Bum, and we're putting up a tree, with lights and decorations, and you're going to get your little brown butt up on the roof and do Frosty."

"No!"

"Yes!"

Another long pause and Luther could hear a clock ticking loudly somewhere in the kitchen. Or perhaps it was the steady pounding of his heart. His shorts caught his attention. Just minutes earlier he'd put them on in anticipation of a magical trip to paradise.

Nora put the phone down and went to the kitchen, where drawers were soon being slammed.

Luther continued staring at his colorful shorts. Now they made him ill. Gone were the cruise, the beaches, the islands, the warm waters, and the nonstop food.

How could one phone call change so much?

Thirteen

··

$\mathcal{L}$uther slowly made his way to the kitchen, where his wife was sitting at the table, lists already under way. "Can we talk about this?" he pleaded.

"Talk about what, Luther?" she snapped.

"Let's tell her the truth."

"Another dumb idea."

"The truth is always better."

She stopped writing and glared at him. "Here's the truth, Luther. We have less than seven hours to get this place ready for Christmas."

"She should've called earlier."

"No, she assumed we'd be here with a tree and gifts

and a party, same as always. Who would ever dream that two otherwise sensible adults would skip Christmas and go on a cruise?"

"Maybe we can still go."

"Another dumb idea, Luther. She's coming home with her fiancé. Is this registering with you? I'm sure they'll be here for at least a week. I hope so anyway. Forget the cruise. You have bigger problems right now."

"I'm not doing Frosty."

"Yes you are. And I'll tell you something else. Blair will never know about the cruise, understand? She'd be crushed if she knew we'd planned it, and that she'd interfered. Do you understand me, Luther?"

"Yes ma'am."

She thrust a sheet of paper at him. "Here's the plan, bozo. You go buy a tree. I'll get down the lights and ornaments. While you're decorating it, I'll hit the stores and see if there's any food left for a party."

"Who's coming to the party?"

"I haven't got that far yet. Now move. And change clothes, you look ridiculous."

"Don't Peruvians have dark skin?" he asked.

Nora froze for a second. They stared at each other, then both looked away. "I guess it doesn't matter now," she said.

"She's not really getting married, is she?" Luther said, in disbelief.

"We'll worry about the wedding if we survive Christmas."

Luther darted to his car, cranked it, backed down the drive quickly, and sped away. Leaving was easy. Returning would be painful.

Traffic got thick in a hurry, and as he sat still he stewed, and fumed, and cursed. A thousand thoughts raced through his overworked brain. An hour earlier he'd been enjoying a restful morning, sipping his third cup of coffee, etc., etc. Now look at him—just another loser lost in traffic while the clock ticked away.

The Boy Scouts sold trees in a Kroger parking lot. Luther skidded to a stop and jumped from his car. There was one Boy Scout, one scoutmaster, one tree. Business was winding down for the season.

"Merry Christmas, Mr. Krank," said the scoutmaster, who looked vaguely familiar. "I'm Joe Scanlon, same guy who brought a tree to your house a few weeks ago."

Luther was listening but he was also staring at the last tree, a crooked spindly dwarf of a pine shrub that had been passed over for good reasons. "I'll take it," he said, pointing.

"Really?"

"Sure, how much?"

A handmade sign leaning against a pickup truck listed various prices, beginning with $75 and falling all the way to $15 as the days had passed. All prices, including the $15, had been scratched through.

Scanlon hesitated, then said, "Seventy-five bucks."

"Why not fifteen?"

"Supply and demand."

"It's a rip-off."

"It's for the Boy Scouts."

"I'll give you fifty."

"Seventy-five, take it or leave it."

Luther handed over the cash and the Boy Scout placed a flattened cardboard box on top of Luther's Lexus. They wrestled the tree up and onto the car, then secured it with rope. Luther watched them carefully, glancing at his watch every two minutes.

When the tree was in place, the hood and trunk were already accumulating dead pine needles, lots of them. "It needs water," said the Scout.

"I thought you weren't doing Christmas," Scanlon said.

"Merry Christmas," Luther said gruffly, getting in his car.

"I wouldn't drive too fast."

"Why not?"

"Those pine needles are awfully brittle."

Back in traffic, Luther sat low behind the wheel and stared straight ahead as he crept along. At a traffic light, a soft drink delivery truck eased next to him and stopped. He heard someone yell, looked up to his left, then cracked his window. A couple of rednecks were staring down, grinning.

"Hey, buddy, that's the ugliest tree I've ever seen!" yelled one.

"It's Christmas, come on, spend some money!" yelled the other, and they roared with laughter.

"That tree's shedding faster than a dog with mange," yelled one of them, and Luther raised his window. Still, he could hear them laughing.

As he neared Hemlock, his pulse quickened. With a little luck, maybe he could make it home without being seen. Luck? How could he hope for good luck?

But it happened. He roared past his neighbors' homes, hit his driveway on two wheels, and came to a sliding stop in the garage. All this without seeing a soul. He jumped from the car and was pulling at the ropes when he stopped, and stared, in disbelief. The tree was completely bare—nothing but crooked limbs and branches, no greenery whatsoever. The brittle pine needles Scanlon had warned him about were still blowing in the wind between the Kroger and Hemlock Street.

The tree was a pitiful sight lying there on the flattened cardboard, dead as driftwood.

Luther looked around, scanned the street, then yanked the tree off the car and pulled it through the garage door and into the backyard where no one could see it. He toyed with the idea of lighting a match and putting it out of its misery, but there was no time for ceremonies.

Thankfully, Nora had already left. Luther stomped into the house and almost crashed into a wall of boxes she'd hauled from the attic—boxes carefully marked: new ornaments, old ornaments, garland, tree lights, outside lights. Nine boxes in all, and he'd been left with the chore of emptying their contents and decorating the tree. It would take days.

What tree!

On the wall by the phone she'd tacked a message with the names of four couples for him to call. All were very close friends, the kind you could confess to and say, "Look, we've screwed up. Blair's coming home. Please forgive us and come to our party."

He'd call them later. But the note said do it now. So he dialed the number for Gene and Annie Laird, perhaps their oldest friends in town. Gene answered the phone and had to yell because a riot was under way. "Grandkids!" he said. "All four of them. Got an extra spot on the cruise ship, old boy?"

Luther gritted his teeth and plowed through a quick narrative, then gave the invitation. "What a bummer!" Gene yelled. "She's coming home now?"

"Right."

"And bringing a Peruvian?"

"You got it. Quite a shock, really. Can you guys help us out?"

"Sorry, pal. We got family in from five states."

"Oh, they're invited too. We need a crowd."

"Let me check with Annie."

Luther slammed down the phone, looked at the nine large boxes, and was hit with an idea. Probably a bad idea, but at the moment good ones were scarce. He ran into the garage and gazed across the street at the Trogdon house. The van was packed with luggage and skis were strapped across the top of it. Wes Trogdon emerged from his garage with a backpack to throw on board. Luther stepped quickly across the Beckers' front lawn and yelled, "Hey, Wes!"

"Hello, Luther," he said hurriedly. "Merry Christmas."

"Yeah, Merry Christmas to you." They met behind Trogdon's van. Luther knew he had to be quick.

"Look, Wes, I'm in a bit of a jam."

"Luther, we're late. We should've been on the road two hours ago." A small Trogdon darted around the van, firing a space gun at an unseen target.

"Just take a minute," Luther said, trying to be cool but hating the fact that he was begging. "Blair called an hour ago. She'll be home tonight. I need a Christmas tree."

The hurried and stressed look on Wes's face relaxed, then a smile broke out. Then he laughed.

"I know, I know," Luther said, defeated.

"What're you going to do with that tan?" Wes asked between laughs.

"Okay, okay. Look, Wes, I need a tree. There are no more trees for sale. Can I borrow yours?"

Trish screamed from somewhere inside the garage, "Wes! Where are you?"

"Out here!" he yelled back. "You want my tree?"

"Yes, I'll return it before you get home. I swear."

"That's ridiculous."

"Yes, it is, but I have no choice. Everybody else'll be using their trees tonight, and tomorrow."

"You're serious, aren't you?"

"Dead serious. Come on, Wes."

Wes pulled a key ring from his pocket and removed the ones to the garage door and the house. "Don't tell Trish," he said.

"I swear I won't."

"And if you break an ornament then we're both dead."

"She'll never know it, Wes, I promise."

"This is funny, you know."

"Why am I not laughing?"

They shook hands, and Luther hurried back to his house. He'd almost made it when Spike Frohmeyer wheeled into his driveway on his bike. "What was that all about?" he demanded.

"I beg your pardon," Luther said.

"You and Mr. Trogdon."

"Why don't you mind your own—" Luther caught himself, and saw opportunity. He needed allies at the moment, not enemies, and Spike was just the type.

"Hey, Spike buddy," he said warmly, "I need a little help."

"What's the deal?"

"The Trogdons are leaving home for a week, and I'm going to keep their tree for them."

"Why?"

"Trees catch on fire a lot, especially ones loaded with lights. Mr. Trogdon is worried about the tree getting too hot, so I'm going to move it over to my house for a few days."

"Just turn the lights off."

"Still got all those wires and stuff. It's pretty dangerous. Think you could give me a hand? I'll pay you forty bucks."

"Forty bucks! You gotta deal."

"We need a small wagon."

"I'll borrow Clem's."

"Hurry. And don't tell anybody."

"Why not?"

"It's part of the deal, okay?"

"Sure. Whatever."

Spike sped away, off on a mission. Luther took a deep breath and gazed up and down Hemlock. Eyes were watching him, he felt sure, the way they'd been peeking at him for weeks now. How did he become such a villain in his own neighborhood? Why was it so hard to dance to his own beat once in a great while? To do something no one had dared? Why all this resentment from people he'd known and liked for years?

Regardless of what happened in the next few hours, he vowed that he would not be reduced to begging his neighbors to come to the party. First, they wouldn't come because they were ticked off. Second, he wouldn't give them the satisfaction of saying no.

Fourteen

....

$\mathcal{H}$is second call was to the
Albrittons, old friends from church who lived an hour away.
Luther spilled his guts, and by the time he finished Riley
Albritton was roaring with laughter. "It's Luther," Riley said
to someone in the background, probably Doris. "Blair just
called. She'll be home tonight." And with that, Doris or
whoever it was broke into hysterics.

Luther wished he hadn't called. "Help me out here,
Riley," he pleaded. "Can you guys stop by?"

"Sorry, bud. We're going to the MacIlvaines for dinner. They invited us a bit earlier, you know."

"All right," Luther said and hung up.

The phone rang immediately. It was Nora, her voice

as edgy as Luther'd ever heard it. "Where are you?" she demanded.

"Well, I'm in the kitchen. Where are you?"

"I'm sitting in traffic on Broad, near the mall."

"Why are you going to the mall?"

"Because I couldn't park at the District, couldn't even get in off the street. I've bought nothing. Do you have a tree?"

"Yes, a real beauty."

"Are you decorating it?"

"Yes, I have Perry Como crooning 'Jingle Bells' in the background while I'm sipping eggnog and trimming our tree. Wish you were here?"

"Have you called anyone?"

"Yes, the Lairds and Albrittons, neither can make it."

"I've called the Pinkertons, Harts, Malones, and Burklands. They're all busy. Pete Hart laughed at me, the bore."

"I'll beat him up for you." Spike was knocking on the door. "I gotta get busy."

"I guess you'd better start calling the neighbors," she said, her hyper voice faltering.

"Why?"

"To invite them."

"Not in a million years, Nora. I'm hanging up now."

"No word from Blair."

"She's on an airplane, Nora. Call me later."

Spike's borrowed wagon was a red Radio Flyer that had seen its better years. With one look, Luther deemed it too small and too old, but they had no choice. "I'll go over first," he explained, as if he knew exactly what he was doing. "Wait five minutes, then bring the wagon over. Don't let anyone see you, okay?"

"Where's my forty bucks?"

Luther handed him a twenty. "Half now, half when the job is done."

He entered the Trogdon home through the side door of the garage, and felt like a burglar for the first time in memory. When he opened the door to the house, an alarm beeped for a few seconds, very long seconds in which Luther's heart froze and his entire life and career flashed before him. Caught, arrested, convicted, his license revoked, banished by Wiley & Beck, disgraced. Then it stopped, and he waited another few seconds before he could breathe. A panel by the rear door said things were Clear.

What a mess. The house was a landfill with debris strewn everywhere, clear evidence of another successful visit by Ole St. Nick. Trish Trogdon would choke her husband if she knew he'd given Luther the keys. In the living room, he stopped and stared at the tree.

It was well known on Hemlock that the Trogdons took little care in decorating their tree. They allowed their children to hang anything they could find. There were a million lights, strands of mismatched garlands, tacky ornaments by the boxload, red and green icicles, even strings of popcorn.

Nora will kill me, Luther thought, but he had no choice. The plan was so simple it had to work. He and Spike would remove the breakable ornaments, and the garlands, and for sure the popcorn, lay them all on the sofa and chairs, ease the tree out of the house with lights intact, haul it over to Luther's, and dress it with real decorations. Then, at some point in the near future, Luther and perhaps Spike would strip it again, haul it across the street, put the Trogdon junk back on it, and everybody would be happy.

He dropped the first ornament and it shattered into a dozen pieces. Spike showed up. "Don't break anything," Luther said, as he cleaned up the ornament.

"Are we getting in trouble for this?" Spike asked.

"Of course not. Now get to work. And fast."

Twenty minutes later the tree was stripped of anything breakable. Luther found a dirty towel in the laundry, and lying flat on his stomach, under the tree, he managed to work the metal tree stand onto the towel. Spike leaned in above him, gently shoving the tree to one side, then the other. On hands and knees, Luther managed to slide the tree toward Spike, across the wood floor, across the tile of the kitchen, down the narrow hall to the laundry, where the branches scraped the walls and dead spruce needles trailed behind.

"You're making a mess," Spike said, helpfully.

"I'll clean it later," said Luther, who was sweating like a sprinter.

The tree, of course, was wider than the door to the garage, as all trees are. Spike pulled the wagon close. Luther grabbed the trunk of the tree, lifted it with a strain, swung the bottom through the door and pulled the whole thing through. When it was sitting safely in the garage, Luther caught his breath, hit the garage door opener, and managed a smile at Spike.

"Why are you so brown?" the kid asked.

The smile vanished as Luther was reminded of the cruise he wouldn't be taking. He looked at his watch—twelve-forty. Twelve-forty and not a single guest for the party, no food, no Frosty, no lights strung anywhere, no tree, as yet, but one on the way. It seemed hopeless at that moment.

You can't quit, old boy.

Luther strained again and lifted the tree up. Spike shoved the wagon under, and of course the metal tree stand was wider than the Radio Flyer. Luther got it balanced, though, and watched it for a moment. "You sit here," he said, pointing to a tiny spot in the wagon and under the tree. "Keep it from tipping over. I'll push."

"You think this'll work?" Spike said, with great suspicion.

Across the street, Ned Becker had been minding his own business when he saw the tree disappear from the Trodgons' front window. Five minutes passed, and the tree reappeared in the open garage, where a man and a kid were wrestling with it. He looked harder, and recognized Luther Krank. Watching every move, he called Walt Scheel on a portable phone.

"Hey, Walt, Ned here."

"Merry Christmas, Ned."

"Merry Christmas, Walt. Say, I'm watching the Trogdons' house, and it appears as if Krank has lost his mind."

"How's that?"

"He's stealing their Christmas tree."

Luther and Spike began their way down the Trogdon

driveway, which had a slight decline to the street. Luther was behind the wagon, hanging on, letting it roll slightly. Spike clutched the trunk of the tree, terrified.

Scheel peeked out his front door, and when he saw the theft with his own eyes, he punched the number for the police.

The desk sergeant answered.

"Yes, this is Walt Scheel, Fourteen eighty-one Hemlock. There's a burglary under way, right now."

"Where?"

"Right here. At Fourteen eighty-three Hemlock. I'm watching it in progress. Hurry."

Trogdon's tree made it across Hemlock to the other side, right in front of the Becker house, where now in the front window Ned, his wife, Jude, and his mother-in-law were watching. Luther negotiated a right turn with the handle, and began pulling the wagon toward his house.

He wanted to sprint before anyone saw him, but Spike kept telling him to take it slow. Luther was afraid to look around, and he didn't believe for a second that he was going unnoticed. When he was almost to his driveway, Spike said, "Cops."

Luther wheeled around just as the patrol car slowed to a stop in the middle of the street, lights flashing but no siren. Two officers jumped out as if it were a SWAT mission.

Luther recognized Salino with the large stomach, then young Treen with the thick neck. The same two who'd stopped by hawking calendars for the Police Benevolent Association.

"Hello, Mr. Krank," Salino said with a smirk.

"Hello."

"Where you going with that?" asked Treen.

"To my house," Luther said, pointing. He'd come so close.

"Maybe you'd better explain," said Salino.

"Yeah, well, Wes Trogdon over there let me borrow his Christmas tree. He left town an hour ago, and me and Spike here were just moving it."

"Spike?"

Luther turned and looked behind him, down at the wagon, at the narrow gap where Spike had been. Spike was gone, nowhere to be seen on Hemlock.

"Yeah, a kid down the street."

Walt Scheel had a seat on the fifty-yard line. Bev was resting, or trying to. His laughter got so loud that she came to see what was the matter. "Pull up a chair, honey, they've caught Krank stealing a tree."

The Beckers were howling too.

"We got a report that a burglary was in progress," said Treen.

"There's no burglary. Who called?"

"A Mr. Scheel. Whose wagon is this?"

"I don't know. Spike's."

"So you stole the wagon too," said Treen.

"I've stolen nothing."

"You have to admit, Mr. Krank, it looks very suspicious," Salino said.

Yes, under normal circumstances, Luther might be forced to say that the entire scene was a bit unusual. But

Blair was getting closer by the minute, and there was no time to back down. "Not at all, sir. I borrow Trogdon's tree all the time."

"We'd better take you in for questioning," Treen said, and unsnapped a pair of handcuffs from his belt. The sight of the silver cuffs sent Walt Scheel to the floor. The Beckers were having trouble breathing.

And Luther went weak at the knees. "Come on, you can't be serious."

"Get in the backseat."

. . .

Luther sat low in the back, thinking of suicide for the first time in his life. The two cops in the front seat were chatting on the radio, something about finding the owner of the stolen property. Their lights were still swirling, and Luther wanted to say so much. Let me go! I'll sue! Turn off the damned lights! Next year I'll buy ten calendars! Just go ahead and shoot me!

If Nora came home now, she'd file for divorce.

The Kirby twins were eight-year-old delinquents from the far end of Hemlock, and for some reason they happened by. They walked close to the car, close to the rear window, and made direct eye contact with Luther, who squirmed even lower. Then the Bellington brat joined them and all three peered in at Luther as if he'd killed their mothers.

Spike came running, followed by Vic Frohmeyer. The officers got out and had a word with him, then Treen shooed the kids away and released Luther from the backseat.

"He's got keys," Vic was saying, and Luther then remembered that he did indeed have the keys to Trogdon's. What a moron!

"I know both these men," Frohmeyer continued. "This is no burglary."

The cops whispered for a moment as Luther tried to ignore the stares from Vic and Spike. He glanced around, half-expecting to see Nora wheel into the drive and have a stroke.

"What about the tree?" Salino asked Vic.

"If he says Trogdon loaned it to him, then that's the truth."

"You sure?"

"I'm sure."

"Okay, okay," Salino said, still sneering at Luther as if he'd never seen a guiltier criminal. They slowly got in the car and drove away.

"Thanks," Luther said.

"What're you doing, Luther?" Vic asked.

"I'm borrowing their tree. Spike's helping me move it. Let's go, Spike."

Without further interruption, Luther and Spike rolled the tree up the driveway, into the garage, and grappled with it until it was sitting rather nicely in the front window. Along the way they left a trail of dead needles, red and green icicles, and some popcorn. "I'll vacuum later," Luther said. "Let's check the lights."

The phone rang. It was Nora, more panicked than before. "I can't find a thing, Luther. No turkey, no ham, no chocolates, nothing. And I can't find a nice gift either."

"Gifts? Why are you shopping for gifts?"

"It's Christmas, Luther. Have you called the Yarbers and Friskis?"

"Yes," he lied. "Their lines were busy."

"Keep calling, Luther, because no one is coming. I've tried the McTeers, Morrises, and Warners, they're all busy. How's the tree?"

"Coming along."

"I'll call later."

Spike plugged in the lights and the tree came to life. They attacked the nine boxes of decorations without a care as to what went where.

Across the street, Walt Scheel watched them through binoculars.

Fifteen

·····································

$\mathcal{S}$pike was on the ladder, leaning precariously into the tree with a crystal angel in one hand and a fuzzy reindeer in the other, when Luther heard a car in the drive. He glanced out the window and saw Nora's Audi sliding into the garage. "It's Nora," he said. Quick thinking led him to believe that Spike's complicity in the tree should be kept a secret.

"Spike, you need to leave, and now," he said.

"Why?"

"Job's over, son, here's the other twenty. Thanks a million." He helped the kid down from the ladder, handed over the cash, and led him to the front door. When Nora stepped into the kitchen, Spike eased onto the front steps and disappeared.

"Unload the car," she commanded. Her nerves were shot and she was ready to snap.

"What's the matter?" he asked, and immediately wished he'd said nothing. It was quite obvious what was the matter.

She rolled her eyes and started to snap, then gritted her teeth and repeated, "Unload the car."

Luther high-stepped toward the door and was almost outside when he heard, "What an ugly tree!"

He spun, ready for war, and said, "Take it or leave it."

"Red lights?" she said, her voice incredulous. Trogdon had used a strand of red lights, one solitary string of them, and had wrapped them tightly around the trunk of the tree. Luther had toyed with the idea of pulling them off, but it would've taken an hour. Instead, he and Spike had tried to hide them with ornaments. Nora, of course, had spotted them from the kitchen.

Now she had her nose in the tree. "Red lights? We've never used red lights."

"They were in the box," Luther lied. He did not enjoy lying, but he knew it would be standard behavior for the next day or so.

"Which box?"

"What do you mean, 'Which box?' I've been throwing stuff on the tree as fast as I can open boxes, Nora. Now's not the time to get touchy about the tree."

"Green icicles?" she said, picking one off the tree. "Where'd you find this tree?"

"I bought the last one from the Boy Scouts." A side-step, not a direct lie.

She looked around the room, at the strewn and empty boxes, and decided there were more important things to worry about.

"Besides," Luther said, unwisely, "at the rate we're going, who's gonna see it?"

"Shut up and unload the car."

There were four bags of food from a store Luther'd never heard of, three shopping bags with handles from a clothing store in the mall, a case of soft drinks, a case of bottled water, and a bouquet of dreadful flowers from a florist known for his outrageous prices. Luther's accountant's brain wanted to tally up the damage, but he thought better of it.

How would he explain this around the office? All the money he'd saved now up in smoke. Plus, the cruise he didn't take getting wasted because he'd declined to purchase travel insurance. Luther was in the middle of a financial disaster and couldn't do a thing to stop the bleeding.

"Did you get the Yarbers and the Friskis?" Nora asked at the phone, the receiver stuck to her head.

"Yes, they can't come."

"Unpack those grocery bags," she demanded, then said into the phone, "Sue, it's Nora. Merry Christmas. Look, we've just had a big surprise over here. Blair's coming home with her fiancé, be here tonight, and we're running around like crazy trying to put together a last-minute party." Pause. "Peru, thought we wouldn't see her till next Christ-

mas." Pause. "Yes, quite a surprise." Pause. "Yes, fiancé."
Pause. "He's a doctor." Pause. "He's from down there somewhere, Peru I think, she just met him a few weeks ago and
now they're getting married, so needless to say we're in
shock. So tonight." Pause.

Luther removed eight pounds of smoked Oregon
trout, all packed in airtight thick cellophane wrappers, the
type that gave the impression the fish had been caught
years ago.

"Sounds like a nice party," Nora was saying. "Sorry
you can't make it. Yes, I'll give a hug to Blair. Merry Christmas, Sue." She hung up and took a deep breath. With the
worst possible timing Luther said, "Smoked trout?"

"Either that or frozen pizza," she fired back with glowing eyes and clenched fists. "There's not a turkey or a ham
left in the stores, and, even if I found one, there's not
enough time to cook it. So, yes, Luther, Mr. Beach Bum,
we're having smoked trout for Christmas."

The phone rang and Nora snatched it.

"Hello, yes, Emily, how are you? Thanks for returning
my call."

Luther couldn't think of a single person named Emily.
He pulled out a three-pound block of Cheddar cheese, a
large wedge of Swiss, boxes of crackers, clam dip, and three
two-day-old chocolate pies from a bakery Nora had always
avoided. She was rattling on about their last-minute party,
when suddenly she said, "You can come! That's wonderful.
Around sevenish, casual, sort of a come-and-go." Pause.
"Your parents? Sure they can come, the more the merrier.

Great, Emily. See you in a bit." She hung up without a smile.

"Emily who?"

"Emily Underwood."

Luther dropped a box of crackers. "No," he said.

She was suddenly interested in unpacking the last bag of groceries.

"You didn't, Nora," he said. "Tell me you didn't invite Mitch Underwood. Not here, not to our house. You didn't, Nora, please say you didn't."

"We're desperate."

"Not that desperate."

"I like Emily."

"She's a witch and you know it. You like her? When's the last time you had lunch with her, or breakfast or coffee or anything?"

"We need bodies, Luther."

"Mitch the Mouth is not a body, he's a windbag. A thundering load of hot air. People hide from the Underwoods, Nora. Why?"

"They're coming. Be thankful."

"They're coming because nobody in their right mind would invite them to a social occasion. They're always free."

"Hand me that cheese."

"This is a joke, right?"

"He'll be good with Enrique."

"Enrique'll never again set foot in the United States after Underwood gets through with him. He hates every-thing—the city, the state, Democrats, Republicans, Independents, clean air, you name it. He's the biggest bore in the world. He'll get half-drunk and you can hear him two blocks over."

"Settle down, Luther. It's done. Speaking of drinking, I didn't have time to get the wine. You'll have to go."

"I'm not leaving the safety of my home."

"Yes, you are. I didn't see Frosty."

"I'm not doing Frosty. I've made up my mind."

"Yes, you are."

The phone rang again, and Nora grabbed it. "Who could this be?" Luther muttered to himself. "Can't get any worse."

"Blair," Nora said. "Hello, dear."

"Gimme the phone," Luther kept muttering. "I'll send 'em back to Peru."

"You're in Atlanta—great," Nora said. Pause. "We're just cooking away, dear, getting ready for the party." Pause. "We're excited too, dear, can't wait." Pause. "Of course I'm making a caramel cream pie, your favorite." She shot Luther a look of horror. "Yes, honey, we'll be at the airport at six. Love you."

Luther glanced at his watch. Three o'clock.

She hung up and said, "I need two pounds of caramel and a jar of marshmallow cream."

"I'll finish the tree—it still needs more ornaments," Luther said. "I'm not fighting the mobs."

Nora chewed a fingernail for a second and assessed things. This meant a plan was coming, probably one with a lot of detail.

"Let's do this," she began. "Let's finish decorating by four. How long will Frosty take?"

"Three days."

"At four, I'll make the final run to town, and you get Frosty up on the roof. Meanwhile, we'll go through the phone book and call everybody we've ever met."

"Don't tell anyone Underwood's coming."

"Hush, Luther!"

"Smoked trout with Mitch Underwood. That'll be the hottest ticket in town."

Nora put on a Sinatra Christmas CD, and for twenty minutes Luther flung more ornaments on Trogdon's tree while Nora set out candles and ceramic Santas and decorated the fireplace mantel with plastic holly and mistletoe. They said nothing to each other for a long time, then Nora broke the ice with more instructions. "These boxes can go back to the attic."

Of all the things Luther hated about Christmas, perhaps the most dreaded chore was hauling boxes up and down the retractable stairs of the attic. Up the staircase to the second floor, then wedge into the narrow hallway between two bedrooms, then readjust positions so that the box, which was inevitably too big, could be shoved up the flimsy ladder through the opening to the attic. Coming down or going up, it didn't matter. It was a miracle he'd avoided serious injury over the years.

"And after that, start bringing Frosty up," she barked like an admiral.

She leaned hard on Reverend Zabriskie, and he finally

said he could stop by for half an hour. Luther, at gunpoint, called his secretary, Dox, and twisted her arm until she agreed to stop by for a few minutes. Dox had been married three times, was currently unmarried but always had a boyfriend of some variety. The two of them, plus Reverend and Mrs. Zabriskie, plus the Underwood group, totaled an optimistic eight, if they all converged at the same time. Twelve altogether with the Kranks and Blair and Enrique.

Twelve almost made Nora cry again. Twelve would seem like three in their living room on Christmas Eve.

She called her two favorite wine stores. One was closed, the other would be open for a half hour. At four, Nora left in a flurry of instructions for Luther, who, by then, was thinking of hitting the cognac hidden in the basement.

Sixteen

....

$\mathcal{J}$ust minutes after Nora left, the phone rang. Luther grabbed it. Maybe it was Blair again. He'd tell her the truth. He'd give her a piece of his mind about how thoughtless this last-minute surprise was, how selfish. She'd get her feelings hurt, but she'd get over it. With a wedding on the way, she'd need them more than ever.

"Hello," he snapped.

"Luther, it's Mitch Underwood," came a booming voice, the sound of which made Luther want to stick his head in the oven.

"Hi, Mitch."

"Merry Christmas to you. Hey, look, thanks for the invite and all, but we just can't squeeze you guys in. Lots of invitations, you know."

Oh yes, the Underwoods were on everyone's A list. Folks clamored for Mitch's insufferable tirades on property taxes and city zoning. "Gee, I'm real sorry, Mitch," Luther said. "Maybe next year."

"Sure, give us a call."

"Merry Christmas, Mitch."

The gathering of twelve was now down to eight, with more defections on the way. Before Luther could take a step, the phone was ringing again. "Mr. Krank, it's me, Dox," came a struggling voice.

"Hello, Dox."

"Sorry about your cruise and all."

"You've already said that."

"Yes, look, something's come up. This guy I'm seeing was gonna surprise me with dinner at Tanner Hall. Champagne, caviar, the works. He made a reservation a month ago. I really can't say no to him."

"Of course you can't, Dox."

"He's hiring a limo, everything. He's a real sweetheart."

"Sure he is, Dox."

"We just can't make it to your place, but I'd love to see Blair."

Blair'd been gone a month. Dox hadn't seen her in two years. "I'll tell her."

"Sorry, Mr. Krank."

"No problem."

Down to six. Three Kranks plus Enrique, and the Reverend and Mrs. Zabriskie. He almost called Nora to break the bad news, but why bother? Poor thing was out there beating her brains out. Why make her cry? Why give her another reason to bark at him for his grand idea gone bad?

Luther was closer to the cognac than he wanted to admit.

. . .

Spike Frohmeyer reported all he'd seen and heard. With forty bucks in his pocket and a fading vow of silence floating around out there, he was at first hesitant to talk. But then no one kept quiet on Hemlock. After a couple of prodding volleys from his father, Vic, he unloaded everything.

He reported how he'd been paid to help take the tree from the Trogdons'; how he'd helped Mr. Krank set it up in his living room, then practically thrown on ornaments and lights; how Mr. Krank had kept sneaking to the telephone and calling people; how he'd heard just enough to know that the Kranks were planning a last-minute party for Christmas Eve, but nobody wanted to come. He couldn't determine the reason for the party, or why it was being put together so hastily, primarily because Mr. Krank used the phone in the kitchen and kept his voice low. Mrs. Krank was running errands and calling every ten minutes.

Things were very tense down at the Kranks', according to Spike.

Vic called Ned Becker, who'd been alerted by Walt

Scheel, and soon the three of them were on a conference call, with Walt and Ned maintaining visual contact with the Krank home.

"She just left again, in a hurry," reported Walt. "I've never seen Nora speed away so fast."

"Where's Luther?" asked Frohmeyer.

"Still inside," answered Walt. "Looks like they've finished with the tree. Gotta say, I liked it better at the Trogdons'."

"Something's going on," said Ned Becker.

. . .

Nora had a case of wine in her shopping cart, six bottles of red and six bottles of white, though she wasn't sure why she was buying so much. Who, exactly, was going to drink it all? Perhaps she would. She'd picked out the expensive stuff too. She wanted Luther to burn when he got the bill. All this money they were going to save at Christmas, and look at the mess they were in.

A clerk in the front of the wine shop was pulling the blinds and locking the door. The lone cashier was hustling the last customers through the line. Three people were ahead of Nora, one behind. Her cell phone rang in her coat pocket. "Hello," she half-whispered.

"Nora, Doug Zabriskie."

"Hello, Father," she said, and began to go limp. His voice betrayed him.

"We're having a bit of a problem over here," he began sadly. "Typical Christmas Eve chaos, you know, everybody running in different directions. And Beth's aunt from Toledo just dropped in, quite unexpected, and made things worse. I'm afraid it will be impossible to stop by and see Blair tonight."

He sounded as if he hadn't seen Blair in years.

"That's too bad," Nora managed to say with just a trace of compassion. She wanted to curse and cry at the same time. "We'll do it another time."

"No problem, then?"

"Not at all, Father."

They signed off with Merry Christmases and such, and Nora bit her quivering lip. She paid for the wine, then hauled it half a mile to her car, grumbling about her husband every heavy step of the way. She hiked to a Kroger, fought her way through a mob in the entrance, and trudged down the aisles in search of caramels.

She called Luther, and no one answered. He'd better be up on the roof.

They met in front of the peanut butter, both seeing each other at the same time. She recognized the shock of red hair, the orange-and-gray beard, and the little, black, round eyeglasses, but she couldn't think of his name. He, however, said, "Merry Christmas, Nora," immediately.

"And Merry Christmas to you," she said with a quick, warm smile. Something bad had happened to his wife, either she'd died from some disease or taken off with a younger man. They'd met a few years earlier at a ball, black tie, she thought. Later, she'd heard about his wife. What was his name? Maybe he worked at the university.

He was well dressed, in a cardigan under a handsome trench coat.

"Why are you out running around?" he asked. He was carrying a basket with nothing in it.

"Oh, last-minute stuff, you know. And you?" She got the impression he was doing nothing at all, that he was out with the hordes just for the sake of being there, that he was probably lonely.

What in the world happened to his wife?

No wedding band visible.

"Picking up a few things. Big meal tomorrow, huh?" he asked, glancing at the peanut butter.

"Tonight, actually. Our daughter's coming in from South America, and we're putting together a quick little party."

"Blair?"

"Yes."

He knew Blair!

Jumping off a cliff, Nora instinctively said, "Why don't you stop by?"

"You mean that?"

"Oh sure, it's a come-and-go. Lots of folks, lots of good food." She thought of the smoked trout and wanted to gag. Surely his name would come back in flash.

"What time?" he asked, visibly delighted.

"Earlier the better, say about seven."

He glanced at his watch. "Just about two hours."

Two hours! Nora had a watch, but from someone else the time sounded so awful. Two hours! "Oh well, gotta run," she said.

"You're on Hemlock," he said.

"Yes. Fourteen seventy-eight." Who was this man?

She scampered away, practically praying that his name would come roaring back from somewhere. She found the caramels, the marshmallow cream, and the pie shells.

The express lane—ten items or less—had a line that stretched down to frozen foods. Nora fell in with the rest, barely able to see the cashier, unwilling to glance at her watch, teetering on the edge of a complete and total surrender.

Seventeen

··

$\mathcal{H}$e waited as long as he could, though he had not a second to spare. Darkness would hit fast at five-thirty, and in the frenzy of the moment Luther had tucked away somewhere the crazy notion of hanging ole Frosty under the cover of darkness. It wouldn't work, and he knew it, but rational thought was hard to grasp and hold.

He spent a few moments planning the project. An attack from the rear of the house was mandatory—no way would he allow Walt Scheel or Vic Frohmeyer or anybody else to see him in action.

Luther wrestled Frosty out of the basement without injuring either one of them, but he was cursing vigorously by the time they made it to the patio. He hauled the ladder from the storage shed in the backyard. So far he had not been seen, or at least he didn't think so.

The roof was slightly wet with a patch of ice or two. And it was much colder up there. With a quarter-inch nylon rope tied around his waist, Luther crawled upward, catlike and terrified, over the asphalt shingles until he reached the summit. He peeked over the crown of the roof and peered below—the Scheels were directly in front of him, way down there.

He looped the rope around the chimney, then inched back down, backward, until he hit a patch of ice and slid for two feet. Catching himself, he paused and allowed his heart to start working again. He looked down in terror. If by some tragedy he fell, he'd free-fall for a very brief flight, then land among the metal patio furniture sitting on hard brick. Death would not be instant, no sir. He'd suffer, and if he didn't die he'd have a broken neck or maybe brain damage.

How utterly ridiculous. A fifty-four-year-old man playing games like this.

The most horrifying trick of all was to remount the ladder from above, which he managed to do by digging his fingernails into the shingles while dangling one foot at a time over the gutter. Back on the ground, he took a deep breath and congratulated himself for surviving the first trip to the top and back.

There were four parts to Frosty—a wide, round base, then a snowball, then the trunk with one arm waving and one hand on hip, then the head with his smiling face, corncob pipe, and black top hat. Luther grumbled as he put the damned thing together, snapping one plastic section into another. He screwed the lightbulb into the midsection, plugged in the eighty-foot extension cord, hooked the nylon rope around Frosty's waist, and maneuvered him into position for the ride up.

It was a quarter to five. His daughter and her brand-new fiancé would land in an hour and fifteen minutes. The drive to the airport took twenty minutes, plus more for parking, shuttling, walking, pushing, shoving.

Luther wanted to give up and start drinking.

But he pulled the rope tight around the chimney, and Frosty started up. Luther climbed with him, up the ladder, worked him over the gutter and onto the shingles. Luther would pull, Frosty would move a little. He was no more than forty pounds of hard plastic but soon felt much heavier. Slowly, they made their way up, side by side, Luther on all fours, Frosty inching along on his back.

Just a hint of darkness, but no real relief from the skies. Once the little team reached the crown, Luther would be exposed. He'd be forced to stand while he grappled with his snowman and attached him to the front of the chimney, and once in place, illuminated with the two-hundred-watt, old Frosty would join his forty-one companions and all of Hemlock would know that Luther had caved. So he paused for a moment, just below the summit, and tried to tell himself that he didn't care what his neighbors thought or said. He clutched the rope that held Frosty, rested on his back and looked at the clouds above him, and realized he was sweating and freezing. They would laugh, and snicker, and tell Luther's skipping Christmas story for years to come, and he'd be the butt of the jokes, but what did it really matter?

Blair would be happy. Enrique would see a real American Christmas. Nora would hopefully be placated.

Then he thought of the *Island Princess* casting off tomorrow from Miami, minus two passengers, headed for the beaches and the islands Luther had been lusting for.

He felt like throwing up.

Walt Scheel had been in the kitchen, where Bev was finishing a pie, and, out of habit now, he walked to his front window to observe the Krank house. Nothing, at first, then he froze. Peeking over the roof, next to the chimney, was Luther, then slowly Walt saw Frosty's black hat, then his face. "Bev!" he yelled.

Luther dragged himself up, looked around quickly as if he were a burglar, braced himself on the chimney, then began tugging on Frosty.

"You must be kidding," Bev said, wiping her hands on a dish towel. Walt was laughing too hard to say anything. He grabbed the phone to call Frohmeyer and Becker.

When Frosty was in full view, Luther carefully swung him around to the front of the chimney, to the spot where he wanted him to stand. His plan was to somehow hold him there for a second, while he wrapped a two-inch-wide canvas band around his rather large midsection and secured it firmly around the chimney. Just like last year. It had worked fine then.

Vic Frohmeyer ran to his basement, where his children were watching a Christmas movie. "Mr. Krank's putting up his Frosty. You guys go watch, but stay on the sidewalk." The basement emptied.

There was a patch of ice on the front side of the roof, just inches from the chimney and virtually invisible to Luther. With Frosty in place but not attached, and while Luther was struggling to remove the nylon rope and pull tight the electrical cord and secure the canvas band around the chimney, and just as he was to make perhaps the most dangerous move of the entire operation, he heard voices below. And when he turned to see who was watching he inadvertently stepped on the patch of ice just below the crown, and everything fell at once.

Frosty tipped over and was gone, careening down the front of the roof with nothing to hold him back—no ropes, cords, bands, nothing. Luther was right behind him, but, fortunately, Luther had managed to entangle himself with everything. Sliding headfirst down the steep roof, and yelling loud enough for Walt and Bev to hear indoors, Luther sped like an avalanche toward certain death.

Later, he would recall, to himself of course, that he clearly remembered the fall. Evidently, there was more ice on the front of the roof than on the rear, and once he found it he felt like a hockey puck. He well remembered flying off the roof, headfirst, with the concrete driveway awaiting him. And he remembered hearing but not seeing Frosty crash somewhere nearby. Then the sharp pain as his fall was stopped—pain around the ankles as the rope and extension cord abruptly ran out of slack, jerking poor Luther like a bullwhip, but no doubt saving his life.

Watching Luther shoot down the roof on his stomach, seemingly in pursuit of his bouncing Frosty, was more than Walt Scheel could stand. He ached with laughter until he bent at the waist. Bev watched in horror.

"Shut up, Walt!" she yelled, then, "Do something!" as Luther was hanging and spinning well above the concrete, his feet not far from the gutter.

Luther swung and spun helplessly above his driveway. After a few turns the cord and rope were tightly braided together, and the spinning stopped. He felt sick and closed his eyes for a second. How do you vomit when you're upside down?

Walt punched 911. He reported that a man had been injured and might even be dying on Hemlock, so send the rescue people immediately. Then he ran out of his house and across the street where the Froymeyer children were gathering under Luther. Vic Frohmeyer was running from two houses down, and the entire Becker clan from next door was spilling out of their house.

"Poor Frosty," Luther heard one of the children say.

Poor Frosty, my ass, he wanted to say.

The nylon rope was cutting into the flesh around his ankles. He was afraid to move because the rope seemed to give just a little. He was still eight feet above the ground, and a fall would be disastrous. Inverted, Luther tried to breathe and collect his wits. He heard Frohmeyer's big mouth. Would somebody please shoot me?

"Luther, you okay?" asked Frohmeyer.

"Swell, Vic, thanks, and you?" Luther began rotating

again, slightly, turning very slowly in the wind. Soon, he pivoted back toward the street, and came face to face with his neighbors, the last people he wanted to see.

"Get a ladder," someone said.

"Is that an electrical cord around his feet?" asked someone else.

"Where is the rope attached?" asked another. All the voices were familiar, but Luther couldn't distinguish them.

"I called nine-one-one," he heard Walt Scheel say.

"Thanks, Walt," Luther said loudly, in the direction of the crowd. But he was revolving back toward the house.

"I think Frosty's dead," one teenager mumbled to another.

Hanging there, waiting for death, waiting for the rope to slip then give completely and send him crashing down, Luther hated Christmas with a renewed passion. Look what Christmas was doing to him.

All because of Christmas.

And he hated his neighbors too, all of them, young and old. They were gathering in his driveway by the dozens now, he could hear them coming, and as he rotated slowly he could glimpse them running down the street to see this sight.

The cord and the rope popped somewhere above him, then gave, and Luther fell another six inches before he was jerked to another stop. The crowd gasped; no doubt, some of them wanted to cheer.

Frohmeyer was barking orders as if he handled these situations every day. Two ladders arrived and one was placed on each side of Luther. Ned Becker yelled from the back patio that he'd found what was holding the electrical cord and the nylon rope, and, in his very experienced opinion, it wouldn't hold much longer.

"Did you plug in the extension cord?" Frohmeyer asked.

"No," answered Luther.

"We're gonna get you down, okay?"

"Yes, please."

Frohmeyer was climbing one ladder, Ned Becker the other. Luther was aware that Swade Kerr was down there, as were Ralph Brixley and John Galdy, and some of the older boys on the street.

My life is in their hands, Luther said to himself, and closed his eyes. He weighed one seventy-four, down eleven for the cruise, and he was quite concerned with how, exactly, they planned to untangle him, then lower him to the ground. His rescuers were middle-aged men who, if they broke a sweat, did so on the golf course. Certainly not power lifting. Swade Kerr was a frail vegetarian who could barely pick up his newspaper, and right then he was under Luther hoping to help lower him to the ground.

"What's the plan here, Vic?" Luther asked. It was difficult to talk with his feet straight above him. Gravity was pulling all the blood to his head, and it was pounding.

Vic hesitated. They really didn't have a plan.

What Luther couldn't see was that a group of men was standing directly under him, to break any fall.

What Luther could hear, though, were two things. First, someone said, "There's Nora!"

Then he heard sirens.

Eighteen

....

The crowd parted to allow the ambulance through. It stopped ten feet from the ladders, from the man hanging by his feet and his would-be rescuers. Two medics and a fireman jumped out, removed the ladders, shooed back Frohmeyer and his cohorts, then one of them drove the ambulance carefully under Mr. Krank.

"Luther, what are you doing up there?" Nora yelled as she rushed through the crowd.

"What does it look like?" he yelled back, and his head pounded harder.

"Are you okay?"

"Wonderful."

The medics and the fireman crawled up on the hood of the ambulance, quickly lifted Luther a few inches, unraveled the cord and the rope, then eased him down. A few folks applauded, but most seemed indifferent.

The medics checked his vitals, then lowered him to the ground and carried him to the back of the ambulance, where the doors were open. Luther's feet were numb and he couldn't stand. He was shivering, so a medic draped two orange blankets over him. As he sat there in the back of the ambulance, looking toward the street, trying to ignore the gawking mob that was no doubt reveling in his humiliation, Luther could only feel relief. His headfirst slide down the roof had been brief but horrifying. He was lucky to be conscious right now.

Let them stare. Let them gawk. He ached too much to care.

Nora was there to inspect him. She recognized the fireman Kistler and the medic Kendall as the two fine young men who'd stopped by a couple of weeks ago selling fruitcakes for their holiday fund-raiser. She thanked them for rescuing her husband.

"You wanna go to the hospital?" asked Kendall.

"Just a precaution," said Kistler.

"No thanks," Luther said, his teeth chattering. "Nothing's broken." At that moment, though, everything felt broken.

A police car arrived in a rush and parked in the street, of course with its lights still flashing. Treen and Salino jumped out and strutted through the crowd to observe things.

Frohmeyer, Becker, Kerr, Scheel, Brixley, Kropp, Galdy, Bellington—they all eased in around Luther and Nora. Spike was in the middle of them too. As Luther sat there, nursing his wounds, answering banal questions from the boys in uniform, practically all of Hemlock squeezed in for a better view.

When Salino got the gist of the story, he said, rather loudly, "Frosty? I thought you guys weren't doing Christmas this year, Mr. Krank. First you borrow a tree. Now this."

"What's going on, Luther?" Frohmeyer called out. It was a public question. Its answer was for everyone.

Luther looked at Nora, and realized she wasn't about to say a word. The explanations belonged to him.

"Blair's coming home, for Christmas," he blurted, rubbing his left ankle.

"Blair's coming home," Frohmeyer repeated loudly, and the news rippled through the crowd. Regardless of how they felt about Luther at the moment, the neighbors adored Blair. They'd watched her grow up, sent her off to college, and waited for her to come back each summer. She'd babysat for most of the younger kids on Hemlock. As an only child, Blair had treated the other children like family. She was everyone's big sister.

"And she's bringing her fiancé," Luther added, and this too swept through the onlookers.

"Who's Blair?" asked Salino, as if he were a homicide detective digging for clues.

"She's my daughter," Luther explained to the uninformed. "She left about a month ago for Peru, with the

Peace Corps, not going to be back for a year, or so we thought. She called around eleven today. She was in Miami, coming home to surprise us for Christmas, and she's bringing a fiancé, some doctor she just met down there." Nora moved closer and was now holding his elbow.

"And she expects to see a Christmas tree?" Frohmeyer said.

"Yes."

"And a Frosty?"

"Of course."

"And what about the annual Krank Christmas Eve party?"

"That too."

The crowd inched closer as Frohmeyer analyzed things. "What time does she get here?" he asked.

"Plane lands at six."

"Six!"

People looked at their watches. Luther rubbed the other ankle. His feet were tingling now, a good sign. Blood was flowing down there again.

Vic Frohmeyer took a step back and looked into the faces of his neighbors. He cleared his throat, raised his chin, and began, "Okay, folks, here's the game plan. We're about to have a party here at the Kranks', a Christmas homecoming for Blair. Those of you who can, drop what you're doing and pitch in. Nora, do you have a turkey?"

"No," she said sheepishly. "Smoked trout."

"Smoked trout?"

"That's all I could find."

Several of the women whispered, "Smoked trout?"

"Who has a turkey?" Frohmeyer asked.

"We have two," said Jude Becker. "Both in the oven."

"Great," said Frohmeyer. "Cliff, you take a team down to Brixley's and get his Frosty. Get some lights too, we'll string 'em along Luther's boxwoods here. Everybody go home, change clothes, grab whatever extra food you can find, and meet back here in a half hour."

He looked at Salino and Treen and said, "You guys head to the airport."

"For what?" asked Salino.

"Blair needs a ride home."

"I'm not sure if we can."

"Shall I call the Chief?"

Treen and Salino headed for their car. The neighbors began to scatter, now that they had their instructions from Frohmeyer. Luther and Nora watched them disperse up and down Hemlock, all moving quickly, all with a purpose.

Nora looked at Luther with tears in her eyes, and Luther felt like crying too. His ankles were raw.

Frohmeyer said, "How many guests are coming to the party?"

"Oh, I don't know," Nora said, staring at the empty street.

"Not as many as you think," Luther said to her. "The Underwoods called and canceled. As did Dox."

"So did Father Zabriskie," said Nora.

"Not Mitch Underwood?" queried Frohmeyer.

"Yes, but he's not coming."

What a sad little party, thought Frohmeyer. "So how many guests do you need?"

"Everybody's invited," Luther said. "The whole street."

"Yes, the entire street," Nora added.

Frohmeyer looked at Kistler and asked, "How many guys in the station tonight?"

"Eight."

"Can the firemen and medics come too?" Vic asked Nora.

"Yes, they're all invited," she said.

"And the police as well," added Luther.

"It'll be a crowd."

"A crowd would be nice, wouldn't it, Luther?" Nora said.

He pulled the blankets tighter and said, "Yes, Blair would love a crowd."

"How about some carolers?" Frohmeyer asked.

"That would be nice," Nora said.

They helped Luther into the house, and by the time he made it to the kitchen he was walking unassisted, but with a severe limp. Kendall left him a plastic cane, one he vowed he wouldn't use.

When they were alone in the living room, with Trogdon's tree, Luther and Nora shared a few quiet moments by the fire. They talked about Blair. They tried in vain to analyze the prospect of a fiancé, then a groom, then a new son-in-law.

They were touched beyond words by the unity of their neighbors. The cruise was never mentioned.

Nora looked at her watch and said she had to get ready. "I wish I'd had a camera," she said, walking away. "You up there hanging by your feet with half the city watching." And she laughed all the way to the bedroom.

Nineteen

....

*B*lair was just a little miffed that her parents were not waiting at the arrival gate. Sure it was short notice, and the airport was crowded, and they were undoubtedly busy with the party, but she was, after all, bringing home her one and only. She said nothing though, as she and Enrique walked quickly down the concourse, arm in arm, stride for stride, somehow weaving gracefully through the mob while remaining attached at the hip and staring only at each other.

There was no one to greet them at the baggage claim either. But as they were hauling their luggage toward the exit, Blair saw two policemen holding a hand-scrawled sign that read "Blair and Enriqe."

They had misspelled Enrique, but at the moment who cared? She called to them, and they snapped into action, scooping up the luggage and leading them through the mass of people. Officer Salino explained as they walked outside that the Chief had dispatched a police escort for Blair and Enrique. Welcome home!

"The party is waiting," he said as they stuffed their things into the trunk of a police car, which was parked illegally at the curb in front of the taxis. A second police car was parked in front of the first.

As a South American, Enrique was more than a little hesitant to voluntarily get into the back of a police car. He looked around nervously, at the crush of foot traffic, taxis, and buses bumper to bumper, people yelling, guards whistling. The idea of bolting crossed his mind, then his eyes returned to the beautiful face of the girl he loved.

"Let's go," she said, and they jumped in. He would've followed her anywhere. With lights flashing, the two cars flew away, darting through traffic, forcing others onto the edges of the streets.

"This happens all the time?" Enrique whispered.

"Never," Blair answered. What a nice touch, she thought.

Officer Treen was driving furiously. Officer Salino was smiling at the thought of Luther Krank hanging by his feet while the entire neighborhood looked on. But he wouldn't say a word. Blair would never know the truth, according to orders from Vic Frohmeyer, who'd finally gotten through to the Mayor and also had the Chief's ear.

As they worked their way into the suburbs, the traffic thinned and a light snow began. "Calling for four inches," Salino said over his shoulder. "Does it snow down in Peru?"

"In the mountains," Enrique said. "But I live in Lima, the capital."

"Had a cousin went to Mexico one time," Salino said, but let it go because there was nothing else to add. The cousin had almost died, etc., but Salino wisely decided not to venture into third-world horror stories.

Blair was determined to be hyperprotective of her fiancé and his homeland, so she quickly rushed in with a "Has it snowed since Thanksgiving?"

The subject of weather was the most common ground of all. "Had two inches a week ago, wasn't it?" Salino said, glancing at Treen, who was driving with white knuckles in a successful attempt to keep his car no more than five feet behind the police car in front of them.

"Four inches," Treen said with authority.

"No, it was two, wasn't it?" Salino argued.

"Four," Treen said, shaking his head, and this irritated Salino.

They finally settled on three inches of snow as Blair and Enrique huddled in the back and looked at the rows of neatly decorated houses.

"Almost there," she said softly. "That's Stanton, Hemlock is next."

Spike was the lookout. He flashed green twice on his Boy Scout signal lantern, and the stage was set.

. . .

Luther limped pitifully into their bathroom, where Nora was putting the finishing touches on her face. For twenty minutes she'd been desperately experimenting with everything she could find—foundations, powders, highlights. Her wonderfully tanned skin was hidden from the neck down, and she was determined to lighten her face.

It wasn't working, though.

"You look emaciated," Luther said, truthfully. Powder was flying around her head.

Luther was in too much pain to worry about his tan. At Nora's suggestion, he was wearing black—black cardigan over a black turtleneck with dark gray slacks. The darker his attire the paler his skin, in her opinion. The cardigan he'd worn only once, and luckily it was one Blair had given him for a birthday. The turtleneck had never been worn, and neither he nor Nora could remember where it came from.

He felt like a Mafia lieutenant.

"Just give it up," he said as she flung bottles and seemed ready to throw one at him.

"I will not," she snapped. "Blair will not know about the cruise, do you understand, Luther?"

"Then don't tell her about the cruise. Tell her your doctor recommended tanning for, uh, which vitamin is it?"

"D, from the sunshine, not a tanning bed. Another stupid idea, Luther."

"Tell her we've had some unseasonably warm weather, been outside a lot, working in the flower beds."

"That's your lie, and it's not going to work. She's not blind. She'll look at your flower beds and see that they haven't been touched in months."

"Ouch."

"Any more bright ideas?"

"We're getting a head start on spring break? Bought a tanning package."

"Very funny."

She brushed by him in a huff, powder trailing behind her. Luther was limping down the hall, with his new plastic cane, toward the crowd in his living room, when he heard someone yell, "Here they come."

Due to a malfunctioning canvas strap, Ralph Brixley was actually holding his own Frosty in place, in front of Luther Krank's chimney, on Luther's roof, in the snow and the cold, when he saw the green flashing light from the end of the street. "Here they come," he yelled down to Krank's patio, where his assistant, Judd Bellington, was waiting by the ladder and trying to repair the strap.

From Ralph's point of view, he watched with some measure of pride (and some measure of frustration because it was cold up there and getting colder) as his neighborhood circled the wagons to help one of its own, even if it was Luther Krank.

A large choir, under the shaky direction of Mrs. Ellen Mulholland, was assembled next to the driveway and began singing "Jingle Bells." Linda Galdy owned a set of handbells, and her hurriedly recruited band began ringing them along with the choir. The front lawn was covered with neighborhood children, all waiting eagerly for Blair and her mysterious new fiancé.

When the police cars slowed in front of the Kranks', a cheer went up, a loud hello from the kids on Hemlock.

"My goodness," Blair said. "What a crowd."

There was a fire truck parked in front of the Beckers' and a large lime-green ambulance in front of the Trogdons', and on cue all their lights began flashing to welcome Blair. When the police cars rolled to a stop in the driveway, Vic Frohmeyer himself yanked open the front door. "Merry Christmas, Blair!" he boomed.

She and Enrique were soon on the front lawn, surrounded by dozens of neighbors while the choir howled away. Blair introduced Enrique, who seemed just a bit bewildered by the reception. They made their way onto the front steps and into the living room, where another cheer went up. At Nora's request, four firemen and three cops stood shoulder to shoulder in front of the tree, trying to block as much of it as possible from Blair's view.

Luther and Nora waited nervously in their bedroom for a private reunion with their daughter, and for a quiet introduction to Enrique.

"What if we don't like him?" Luther mumbled, sitting on the edge of the bed, rubbing his ankles. The party was growing rowdy down the hall.

"Hush, Luther. We raised a smart girl." Nora was applying a last-minute layer of powder to her cheeks.

"But they just met."

"Love at first sight."

"That's impossible."

"Maybe you're right. It took me three years to see your potential."

The door opened and Blair rushed in. Nora and Luther both glanced at her first, then quickly looked beyond to see how dark Enrique was.

He wasn't dark at all! At least two shades lighter than Luther himself!

They hugged and squeezed their daughter as if she'd been gone for years, then, with great relief, met their future son-in-law.

"You guys look great," Blair said, sizing them up. Nora was wearing a bulky Christmas sweater, the first time in memory that she wanted to look heavier. Luther was the aging gigolo.

"Been watching our weight," he said, still pumping Enrique's hand.

"You've been in the sun," Blair said to Luther.

"Well, yes, we've had some unseasonably warm weather, actually. Got a bit burned in the flower beds last weekend."

"Let's get to the party," Nora said.

"Can't keep folks waiting," Luther added, leading the way.

"Isn't he handsome?" Blair whispered to her mother. Enrique was just a step ahead.

"Very handsome," Nora said proudly.

"Why is Daddy limping?"

"Hurt his foot. He's fine."

The living room was packed with people, a different sort of crowd, Blair noticed, not that it mattered. Most of the regulars were not there. Most of the neighbors were. And she couldn't figure out why the police and firemen had been invited.

There were some gifts for Enrique, which he opened in the center of the room. Ned Becker passed along a red golf shirt from a local country club. John Caldy had just been given a picture book of local country inns. His wife rewrapped it, and they unloaded it on Enrique, who was moved almost to tears. The firemen gave him two fruit-cakes, though he confessed they didn't have such delights down in Peru. The Police Benevolent Association gave him a calendar.

"His English is perfect," Nora whispered to Blair.

"Better than mine," she whispered back.

"I thought you said he'd never been to the U.S."

"He was educated in London."

"Oh." And Enrique went up another notch. Handsome, educated abroad, a doctor. "Where did you meet him?"

"In Lima, during orientation."

A cheer went up as Enrique opened a tall box and removed a lava lamp, one passed along by the Bellingtons.

When the gifts were done, Luther announced, "Dinner," and the crowd moved to the kitchen, where the table was covered with the Hemlock donations, though the food had been arranged and rearranged until it looked original and festive. Even Nora's smoked trout had been dressed up by Jessica Brixley, perhaps the best chef on the street.

The carolers were frozen and tired of the snow, though it wasn't heavy. They heard the news about dinner, and moved inside, along with Mrs. Linda Galdy's handbell ensemble.

The man with the orange-and-gray beard Nora'd met by the peanut butter at Kroger appeared from nowhere and seemed to know everyone, though no one seemed to know him. Nora welcomed him and watched him carefully, and finally heard him introduce himself as Marty somebody. Marty loved a gathering and quickly warmed to the occasion. He cornered Enrique over cake and ice cream, and the two immediately launched into an extended conversation, in Spanish no less.

"Who is that?" Luther whispered as he limped by.

"Marty," Nora whispered back, as if she'd known him for years.

When everyone had eaten, they drifted back to the living room, where a fire was roaring. The children sang two carols, then Marty stepped forward with a guitar. Enrique stepped forward too and explained that he and his new friend would like to sing a couple of traditional Peruvian Christmas songs.

Marty attacked the guitar with a vengeance, and the duet began in a nice harmony. The words were unknown to the audience, but the message was clear. Christmas was a time of joy and peace around the world.

"He sings too," Nora whispered to Blair, who just radiated.

Between songs, Marty explained that he'd once worked in Peru, and that singing the songs made him miss the place. Enrique took the guitar, strummed a few chords, then softly began another carol.

Luther leaned on the mantel, alternating one foot at a time, smiling gamely, though he wanted to lie down and sleep forever. He looked at the faces of his neighbors, all of whom were entranced with the music. They were all there, except for the Trogdons.

And except for Walt and Bev Scheel.

Twenty

··

$\mathscr{A}$fter yet another foreign carol, and during a boisterous round of applause for the Enrique and Marty duet, Luther slipped unnoticed from the kitchen and eased through the darkness of his garage. Dressed in snow attire—overcoat, wool cap, muffler, boots, gloves—he shuffled along, aided by the plastic cane he'd vowed not to use, trying not to wince with each step, though both ankles were swollen and raw.

The cane was in his right hand, a large envelope in his left. The snow was still light, but the ground was covered.

At the sidewalk, he turned and gazed upon the gathering in his living room. A packed house. A tree that improved with the distance. Above them a borrowed Frosty.

Hemlock was quiet. The fire truck and ambulance and police cars were gone, thankfully. Luther looked east and west and saw not a single person moving about. Most of them were in his house, singing along now, rescuing him from an episode that would undoubtedly be remembered as one of his more curious.

The Scheel house was well lit on the outside, but almost completely dark within. Luther crept up their driveway, his boots rubbing his wounds, the cane making the entire venture possible. On their porch he rang the doorbell and looked again at his house directly across the street. Ralph Brixley and Judd Bellington came around the corner, hurriedly stringing lights on Luther's boxwoods.

He closed his eyes for a second, shook his head, looked at his feet.

Walt Scheel answered the door with a pleasant "Well, Merry Christmas, Luther."

"And Merry Christmas to you," Luther said with a genuine smile.

"You're missing your party."

"Just have a second, Walt. Could I step in?"

"Of course."

Luther limped into the foyer, where he parked himself on a matt. His boots had accumulated snow and he didn't want to leave tracks.

"Can I take your coat?" Walt asked. Something was baking in the kitchen, and Luther took that as a good sign.

"No, thanks. How's Bev?"

"She's having a good day, thanks. We started to come

over and see Blair, but the snow started. So how's the fiancé?"

"A very nice young man," Luther said.

Bev Scheel entered from the dining room and said
hello and Merry Christmas. She was wearing a red holiday
sweater and looked the same, as far as Luther could tell.
Rumor was that her doctor had given her six months.

"A pretty nasty fall," Walt said with a smile.

"Could've been worse," Luther said, grinning, trying
to enjoy himself as the butt of the joke. We won't dwell on
that subject, he declared to himself.

He cleared his throat and said, "Look, Blair's here for
ten days, so we won't be taking the cruise. Nora and I
would like for you guys to have it." He lifted the envelope
slightly, sort of waved it at them.

Their reaction was delayed as glances were ex-
changed, thoughts were attempted. They were stunned,
and for quite a spell couldn't speak. So Luther plowed
ahead. "The flight leaves at noon tomorrow. You'll need to
get there early to get the names changed and such, a slight
hassle, but it'll be worth it. I've already called my travel
agency this afternoon. Ten days in the Caribbean, beaches,
islands, the works. It'll be a dream vacation."

Walt shook his head no, but just slightly. Bev's eyes
were moist. Neither could speak until Walt managed to say,
with little conviction, "We can't take it, Luther. It's not
right."

"Don't be silly. I didn't purchase the travel insurance,
so if you don't go then the entire package is wasted."

Bev looked at Walt, who was already looking at her, and when their eyes locked Luther caught it. It was crazy, but why not?

"I'm not sure my doctor will allow it," she said feebly.

"I've got that Lexxon deal on the front burner," Walt mumbled to himself as he scratched his head.

"And we promised the Shorts we'd be there New Year's Eve," Bev added, sort of musing.

"Benny said he might drop in." Benny was their oldest son, who hadn't been home in years.

"And what about the cat?" Bev asked.

Luther let them shuffle and strain, and when they ran out of their flimsy excuses he said, "It's a gift from us to you, a sincere, heart-felt, no-strings-attached Christmas offering to two people who are, at this very moment, having a difficult time finding an excuse. Just go for it, okay?"

"I'm not sure I have the right clothes," Bev said predictably.

To which Walt replied, "Don't be ridiculous."

With their resistance crumbling, Luther moved in for the kill. He shoved the envelope at Walt. "It's all here—airline tickets, cruise passes, brochures, everything, including the phone number of the travel agency."

"What's the cost, Luther? If we go, then we'll reimburse you."

"It's a simple gift, Walt. No cost, no payback. Don't make it complicated."

Walt understood, but his pride got in his way. "We'll just have to discuss it when we get back."

There, they were already gone and back.

"We can talk about everything then."

"What about the cat?" Bev asked.

Walt pinched his chin in serious thought and said, "Yes, that's a real problem. Too late to call the kennel."

With uncanny timing, a large black furry cat sneaked into the foyer, rubbed itself on Walt's right leg, then gave a long look up at Luther.

"We can't just leave him," Bev was saying.

"No, we can't," Walt said.

Luther hated cats.

"We could ask Jude Becker," Bev said.

"No problem. I'll take care of him," Luther said, swallowing hard, knowing perfectly well that Nora would get the chore.

"Are you sure?" Walt asked, a little too quickly.

"No problem."

The cat took another look at Luther and slunk away. The feeling was mutual.

The good-byes took much longer than the hellos, and when Luther hugged Bev he thought she would break. Under the bulky sweater was a frail and ailing woman. The tears were halfway down her cheeks. "I'll call Nora," she whispered. "Thanks."

Old tough-as-nails Walt had moist eyes too. On the front steps, during their last handshake, he said, "This means so much, Luther. Thank you."

When the Scheels were once again locked away inside, Luther started home. Unburdened by the thick envelope now, shed of its pricey tickets and thick brochures, freed of all the self-indulgence contained therein, his steps were a little quicker. And, filled with the satisfaction of making the perfect gift, Luther walked straight and proud with hardly a limp.

At the street he stopped and looked over his shoulder. The Scheels' home, dark as a cave just moments earlier, was now alive with lights being flipped on both upstairs and down. They'll pack all night, Luther thought to himself.

A door opened across the street, and the Galdy family made a noisy exit from the Kranks' living room. Laughter and music escaped with them and echoed above Hemlock. The party showed little signs of breaking up.

Standing there at the edge of the street, light snow gathering on his wool cap and collar, gazing at his freshly decorated house with almost the entire neighborhood packed into it, Luther paused to count his blessings. Blair was home, and she'd brought with her a very nice, handsome, polite young man, who was quite obviously crazy about her. And who, at that moment, was very much in charge of the party along with Marty Whatshisname.

Luther himself was lucky to be standing, as opposed to lying peacefully on a slab at Franklin's Funeral Home, or pinned to a bed in ICU at Mercy Hospital, tubes running everywhere. Thoughts of snowballing down his roof, headfirst, still horrified him. Very lucky indeed.

Blessed with friends and neighbors who would sacrifice their plans for Christmas Eve to rescue him.

He looked up to his chimney where the Brixleys'

Frosty was watching him. Round smiling face, top hat, corncob pipe. Through the flurries Luther thought he caught a wink from the snowman.

Starving, as usual, Luther suddenly craved smoked trout. He began trekking through the snow. "I'll eat a fruitcake too," he vowed to himself.

Skipping Christmas. What a ridiculous idea.

Maybe next year.